# Soledad and The Sea

## a novel

# Soledad and The Sea

Emmanuel Cervantes Mejia

Chusma House Publications

ISBN: 978-0-692-67388-1

cafeofwords.com

Edited by Jennifer M. Glover

Chusma House Publications
PO Box 467
San Jose, CA 95103

**For the Lonely...**
**Also for my loving parents and siblings who**
**always give me their unconditional love and support.**


And a special Thank You to Charley B. Trujillo for being a role model and inspiration but most importantly, for being a friend. Thank you for making this publication possible.

# Part One

The most grandiose of days were those of the sun. My brother and i enjoyed our time within the spring breeze and then a shelter of stars. Life is spent better in our youth; our innocence was the essence of our existence.

i try to recapture vague and distant memories. i remember a game we used to play. We would hold a handful of dandelions and release them into the breeze as high as we could with our eyes closed. On the count of three, we would open our eyes and try to catch as many floating florets as we could. Beams of sunlight would pass through each inverted umbrella, casting a million shadows on the green grass and daisies. The florets floated in the wind like memories as my brother and i chased them as if they were dreams.

We never counted the stems we captured from the wind's grasp, so i lack the memory of us ever arguing or crying. Perhaps it was a time before either of us knew how to count, but it was a grand time no less. Those were the times when we were boys of seven and five. i being the younger of the two, never thought i would ever catch up and eventually pass my brother in age. That time came and passed when i was sixteen. My poor brother, he had allegedly overdosed on prescribed anti-depressants and alcohol when he was just a child of eighteen.

i couldn't cry at his funeral, or maybe i did, i can't be sure. i stood about ten feet from him at the viewing. He always suffered in silence; i never saw him weep or complain. The shadows were the only witnesses, for i would be able to hear his teardrops in most midnight hours. Even when his mood was displayed in the somber veil that masked a young face and a gentle curious smile and gaze, i knew he suffered from something unworldly. i hoped that he would find the peace in death that he could not be granted in his young life. i too, had somewhat lost comfort in believing that a higher power had control of every aspect of our lives. i hoped that his musical hobbies would be available to him up in the clouds or deep in the earth. Amongst literature and poetry was where he found even a tad bit of peace in his melancholy world. These thoughts and hopes exhausted my young mind. Now, years later, eight to be exact, i had come to the conclusion that this illness was hereditary. My mother, to mention the least, cried immensely until the day she passed, a few weeks after my brother. i, too, felt a void and the sense of abandonment i 'm sure my brother and mother felt at their final hour. Yet, eight years later, i find myself trying to function as i share in their distress born of genetics and dreamers' souls. It wasn't until my mother's funeral that i realized that, like my brother and my mother, there isn't a cure for melancholy illnesses. People can't be cured, they die.

These thoughts and memories came to me as i stood over the sea on the ledge of a drop-off. The black jagged rocks glittered sunlight back at me, blinding me. My nose was highly stimulated by the cool and salty breeze that wrapped around me every second that i stood there. The waves crashed on the rocks, but inland, the roar of the sea was the weeping of *La Llorona*—her ghostly elegy metered by the stone beach-head. i glanced down off the cliff and watched the sharp and silky black rocks get smothered by the blue-gray, foamy sea. The rocks greedily grabbed at my attention; they were so dangerously tempting. The waves crashed harder and distracted me from my thoughts. i looked back down at the waves; my eyes slowly caressed the sea's waves out to its horizon. i lit a cigarette. The sight gave me nostalgia, a form of denial, but i thought mainly about what the point of it all was? What was existence and the meaning behind it? i never really had goals; i only dreamt. i never sought acceptance; i accepted our condition, and i never sought answers, for i had no use for them. All i could do was love. This love had melancholy roots. I loved the sea, books and the moon, but i suffered from unrequited love. i wanted and sought to love life, but the unrequited love left my heart to attract and eventually to conform to misfortune. Yes, one can have a little bit of money, but happiness is of a philosophical nature. i sought the meaning of this absurd life while hoping not to find an absurd meaning.

The only reason i wanted to become a writer was because we're all going to die. It didn't make much sense to me to put all the effort into things that would die. Words on a page seemed to never cease as every man before me did and every man eventually will.  i loved and still love my family, yet i find myself alone in my times of need. People die, flowers die. But love doesn't seem to die; love continues to grow until it itself kills a person. Very much like a mushroom that grows upon a tree that is slowly dying. Nonetheless, as the tree slowly dies, it is best to look up at the passing gray and white clouds.

My phone rang. "Damn it." i placed my cigarette between my lips and grabbed my phone from my pant pocket. It was Conor, my agent.

"Conor."

"Johnny Espiritu; how's it going?"

"Awful."

"I'm doing great as well thank you for asking. How's the novel coming along?"

"Peachy."

"Johnny, you're my favorite writer, and I'm your biggest fan. My boss is nagging me. It's been three years since your last publication, and you haven't given us a single page."

"i'm working on it."

"Can you have at least a synopsis in a month from now?"

"Sure," i stalled.

i was affronted when he pressed, "You promise?"

i didn't like to promise anything. The very thought of promising something, or anything for that matter, brings a lot of negativity to my mind. Like a doctor who gets asked to promise that their terminal patient is not going to die. It's an insult to humanity to lie to a person in that manner.

i said, "i promise," and hung up.

i gave my back to the sea and the ledge that i had been standing at for what seemed to be hours and headed to my hotel that was just across the street from Davenport Beach. i grabbed my portable Smith–Corona typewriter and headed down to the front desk to check out. It was supposed to be a weekend getaway just to be able to write, and i, once again, left the hotel with the bitter taste of procrastination and wine on my breath.

~~~~~

i hopped on a train home; what a damn predicament i'd gotten myself into.

It's been about three years since i published my novel, "*Vellichor,*" and about four years since i've written a goddamn predicate. As a child and teenager, i wanted and aspired to be a pugilist and only wrote to pass the time. It wasn't until i started living on my own, when i was eighteen, that i turned my ambitions to writing. i was granted attributes of pugilists: Lamotta's chin, Johnny Tapia's heart, but ill-fated hands. i hurt my hands and needed to do something else, so i became a writer.

i unlocked the front door of my studio apartment in the outskirts of San Jose, a block from the quiet suburbs. It was cozy and had the essentials: my futon that served as my bed and only couch, my bookshelf that wore a three-piece suit made of the old Classics, along with Camus, Kerouac, Steinbeck, that was sown together with Hammett and Chandler. My coffee stained desk faced my only window and was covered by a row of books, notebooks, and barely enough room for my typewriter. Across the studio, up against the wall were my abandoned passions. Paintings i did to pass time and my brother's acoustic guitar. We both learned to play on that guitar, but the music didn't appeal to me like before. Books helped with my occupation but were a constant reminder of my loneliness. Music, however, strung a profound chord of sadness in my chest. I loved the *Rancheras* and even the Rock 'N' Roll, yet for some odd reason, i could barely take it and prefer for my record player to collect dust along with my memories amongst the records i've played.

The silence and calm of my home encouraged my solitude yet assaulted my natural need for company. i didn't hate people; i had an urge to be left alone with my thoughts and sensibilities. For years, if not from early childhood, i was at the mercy of my heart and the tyranny of my emotions. i loved, but i loved in the stillness of life. This love was not the commercialized type of love; my love was for humanity, and the hurt was for the void of meaning in our existence. i looked at the people as i gazed out the window, and all i could see and feel was sorrow.

Tempted, i thought of where i had placed my little black book of contacts—not contacts of cold women but of those of both sexes that i had once called friends. i always used that word loosely, for in my years i couldn't find or couldn't trust one of these people to be as sincere and as simple as the word would imply. i hesitated for not a moment longer and succumbed to my curiosity of their present state. i walked over to a corner table that was right

7

next to my futon and searched through the wooden cabinets. The drawers would creak and were filled with empty miniature bottles of liquor, papers and empty packs of cigarettes. Beneath the collections of false pleasures is where i found my little black book of contacts. i flipped through the pages like a child with a flipbook of a figurine throwing a rock drawn on post-it notes.

i was greeted by pale and virgin pages that were paler than the moon on a summer night and untouched like a rose petal. Then it hit me, struck me harder than i could imagine. i had worn out any form of friends i might have had, or perhaps it was i that had been smoked to the filter and flicked onto the cold ground. If one places all their hopes and self-respect upon another, one will end up sadly disappointed. My eyes glazed over this conclusion.

The concept of suicide troubled me. The suicidal thoughts and urges were, in some way or another, a means that got me through most nights. i was constantly feeling comfort with these terrible nightmares; i turned to writing, cigarettes and the bottle to medicate. Yes, i had once medicated with the company of friends, however, these "friends" could never be found on the darkest and coldest of nights. Friends have a way of driving us to suicide. The wine flowed like the Nile, and i indulged my never-ending thirst every morning and every night. But friends don't flow like the Nile, they hover like bees: from flower to flower, in hopes of pollinating them. But i, being like a weed, have a hard time with pollination. It doesn't serve a need to me. However, i enjoyed the idea and thought that my only need was the hot sun to shine down on me—for its hot beams of light to hold me tenderly like a mother would a newborn. Every time i felt the hot sun shine down on me, i felt like i was embraced by it.

It was under the hot sun where i realized the

concept of friendship was absurd. It is true, man has a natural urge for company or romantic companionship, but it should also be noted that when one feels the most alone, it is often the time when we are without solitude. This i felt was the truth. i've never felt lonely being alone on a Saturday night. Loneliness was felt when i used to surround myself with happy people or being at a boxing match with the crowd cheering on the two boxers to continue battering each other. That's where i felt the loneliest. Everyone on their feet cheering, screaming, drinking beer and forgetting their worries, while i sat quietly watching the poor young men beating the life out of each other. This was absurd, not the boxing match, but the feelings i endured while attending a sporting event with the friends i had at the time. They didn't care, nor did i. i felt like i did love my friends, but i believed there was a fine line between loving and caring. i, too, was at fault. i had loved but not cared; this is where the absurdity lies. No one is innocent; everyone is at fault. Some care but lack love. This too, i found through my experience with friends. At the moment when one needs something, a favor for example, the person in need cares for the friendship, yet the love needed to keep in touch with the friend after the good deed has been done is nonexistent. The absurdity of friendship is not measured by our inability to care for one another; it is measured by our decision not to.

i received another call from Conor. i didn't pay much attention to what he had to say. i knew it was about writing or my lack of writing. i never cared too much for the business side of things; unfortunately, as a writer, one is often pressured by the means of making money; sometimes for personal gain, yet more often for someone else's gain. i kept giving him one-word answers to keep him happy, thinking I was actually paying attention to him. i lit a cigarette. Then i heard him say it, "He's not very happy with you."

"He's not very happy with me?" i thought. The guy who probably never read my book is unhappy with the fact that I haven't been able to make him more money? That's another absurdity. i got hung up with the word "happy." i came to the conclusion that it didn't matter whether or not others were happy around me, what mattered was my happiness. i hadn't felt happy or a sense of happiness since i convinced myself that my mother's suffering had ceased when she died. i wasn't happy i lost my mother, but if her suffering was as terrible as it seemed, i had hoped death brought her happiness. i often felt that my brother, mother and father were happy together wherever they had gone. Times like those, i think of joining them. After all, i wasn't too convinced that happiness was tangible even with all the money and all the time in the world.

i had the means and tools to take my own life. My means were my inability to cope with anything nor to even see the beauty in the sea, flowers, art and even music. i wasn't happy, but what is happiness? Is it a wife and children? Is it money? Is it the everyday chance to be a better person? None of it really mattered to me anymore. The tools i had were a bottomless drum of bourbon and at least a six-month supply of lithium i was supposed to be taking. The early evening had started to fall, and out of laziness, i dropped the idea to off myself and decided to have a cup of coffee and clean my home.

i cleaned everything, even what didn't need cleaning. i vigorously cleaned the countertop as i smoked a cigarette, leaving ashes everywhere. i looked around; cleaning didn't matter. A vase on my windowsill aroused my eye. i hadn't noticed the vase before. There were six dried up red roses; i had no clue where the other six had gone or if they had existed. i walked over and picked up the vase; there was a circular spot of cleanliness on the dusty windowsill. i smelled the roses, taking a deep inhale. i couldn't really smell anything except bitterness. "i should throw them out," i thought to myself, but i decided to keep them. i placed them on my chimney mantle. i lit another cigarette as i sat and drank a glass of wine and embraced the silence that inhabited my home. There was a moment of calmness in my head but a lack of clarity. "i should kill myself to end the debate," i mused. i decided to hit the streets, but not to a club or bar. i decided to take a walk. Whether suicide is an option, or only hope, it is undoubtedly a decision to make after a walk.

~~~~~

i got somewhat dressed up. i didn't like luxury but i appreciated elegance. This trait came about as i lived in nostalgia of a time i never knew. i didn't shower, but i should have. Depression has a way of doing that to people. i dressed mainly in black. Black shoes, black pants, black sports coat and my black paperboy cap. i grabbed my pack of cigarettes, keys and an uncolored attitude and walked out the door.

i walked down a street of a main strip that had rows and rows of rowdy bars and clubs. The sea of cars, their horns and growling engines gave me an anxiety where only a cigarette kept me grounded and able to continue exploring the night.

The sense of loneliness drifted back. i felt it compressing my chest; it made it heavy and affected my breathing. The smoking probably didn't help, but i took deep inhales of my cigarette as i walked the streets. i wasn't comfortable, not with the environment nor my core misery, which i've heard if we are comfortable in either one, it would be a form of happiness. i decided to get away from the main strip. My anxiety got too possessive of my independence.

i took a stroll on the outskirts of the restless nightlife of the downtown area. i smoked countless cigarettes as i watched every passerby with the most kindness of heart. i felt envious. They all walked the streets under the pale moon as they all made their way into the restaurants, cafes and bars. They all seemed to care an awful lot for these destinations as if those were the places where the lost wondered. i took a deep inhale of my cigarette along with the cool night air. i stopped in front of a mom and pop bookstore on the corner of hope and a dead-end called "Soledad's Books and Coffee." i haven't stepped foot in this shop since i had my book signing party three years ago. i took one last puff of my cigarette, put it out and went inside. i was greeted by the smell of fresh coffee being brewed although no one was behind the counter brewing it. The smell of gray-haired books also mixed with the air along with pomade and hairspray. The streets and bars were crawling with the souls of the Saturday nightlife yet the hushed store lived up to its owner's name.

i passed the aisles and rows of books, running my calloused finger tips of my left hand over the sea of pages and words that inhabited the shelves. The lone memory of my book signing came to my mind; the small crowd of people that came in to hear me speak about myself almost brought a form of nostalgia. However, i felt the pain and desolation the sea of words found itself in. Words, although immortal, can cease in the memories of others.

i walked over to the little counter of the café in the middle of the store and looked around. Not a soul could be found. i scouted the place like a bloodhound to no avail. i went around the counter and grabbed a heavy paper cup and helped myself to some hot black coffee. i took a sip and then decided i wanted a little bit of milk. No sugar, for i was sweet enough. i went back around the counter, placed my cup down and reached in my inside pocket of my coat. i placed two single dollar bills on the counter and one dollar in the tip jar, my mother taught my brother and i good manners.

i sipped my coffee as i glanced through the fiction. i found myself on the shelf. i was near to the gnarly Chuck Bukowski. Nonetheless, my ego stepped in and i picked up a copy of my book; i glanced through the pages then was distracted with a movement i caught from the corner of my eye. i turned my head and saw what seemed to be the presence of a heavenly ghost; she smiled at me and then made her way behind the checkout counter. i hated confrontation even if was a friendly greeting by a bartender that is meant to hear all our bullshit. i looked at the time, they were about to close, plus i didn't really need another book but something came over me. Without a glance i grabbed a book; it turned out to be the collection of poetry by the sympathetic Jack Kerouac. Confounded, this was a delight. i headed to the checkout counter and slowed my pace as i approached her.

She was standing behind the counter but her downward gaze had its full attention to a book; i couldn't see the cover. i reached her; she turned her attention towards me and let out a smile. Her beauty mystified me, although, the word "beauty" couldn't be used to describe the angelic essence that radiated from the countenance she wore. i stood in front of her at the counter; book and cup of coffee in hand. She just smiled, as if waiting for me to introduce myself. i placed the book on the counter.

A very relaxed "hello" was the only damn thing that came out of me. i found myself adrift in her clear hazel eyes and dark lovely, wavy hair that flowed past her shoulders. She was dressed quite elegantly for working at a bookstore, but this i found to be marvelous. i myself rarely thought twice of something that i was to wear; even at my book signings and literary events, i often wore a black sport coat and reeked of cigarettes and whiskey. From where i stood, i could smell her perfume. Her perfume excited my nostrils just as much if not more than the sea that was my first love. Her perfume was fruity, sweeter than wine; i wanted to compliment her in some way or form but found myself dumbfounded by the hurt in her smile. She was so lively in a place where she was surrounded by forgotten words and the reality that a genuine friend couldn't be found within miles.

This in a way made me bitter and completely conscious of my self-imposed desolation. Even standing there with her changed the environment; i believed that she herself had changed the smell of the place from smelling like a sullen bookstore, into a garden in the spring. Like a garden in the spring with its cool, chilly morning dew evaporating as the hot sun bathes the cold earth with its grandeur element of infatuation. The chirps from the birds greet the sun—appreciative of it as the cold morning begins to warm. The cool and variant shadows shift around and dance as the flowers turn their heads towards the sun. i realized that when one lives amongst the shadows, we miss out on the sun in more ways than just the abandonment of light.

She grabbed the book as i handed it to her. Her hand lightly touched mine, and i felt the warmth of her soft fingers ascend my arm and burn my chest. Like when you grab a stick and play with the logs of a campfire, you have a moment of fear and excitement and then want to get closer to the fire.

14

"Jack Kerouac?" she queried with curiosity

"You like him?" i probed.

"To be honest, I haven't heard of him. Is he good?"

"He's one of my favorites to say the least."

She didn't say anything; then again she didn't have to. Her gaze said a million words, and that very moment i knew i wanted to read those million words. She gazed down at the book as she flipped through the pages. Her face and gaze were tender, almost maternal. As she glanced up at me, i saw and felt the torrid spirit that possessed her; it radiated from her calmness, her hands as she handled the book, her slight smile and even more in her laugh and from her soul.

The air in the dead room grew denser; i heard the cries from all the forgotten souls roaring from the shelves. Each gasp of air only intensified their laments and their solitude. My palms got clammy. Speechless and embarrassed, i had to leave. i paid for the book and left without it. As soon as i stepped outside, the cold wind from the Saturday stung my lungs. i lit a cigarette to only complicate my breathing even further. i sipped my coffee as i tried to figure out what came over me. i knew i should wait for her to exit so i could excuse myself, although i had no idea how to do so without being viewed as a creep or nuisance.

i stood a good distance from the front door of the solitary bookstore when she finally came out and locked the front door. She was just as stunning the second time seeing her as the first. i puffed my cigarette and approached her. Only a few minutes had passed before she came out. When she sensed me nearing her, she turned and faced me.

"Oh, did you come back for the book?" She put her hand back on the door handle with intentions of re-opening it. i was quick to answer and exhaled my smoke through my nostrils.

"No, i'm here to see you."

i stood there with my cigarette and coffee in hand. i took one last inhale and put my cigarette out.

She smiled in disbelief and asked, "Really?" She smiled one last time and gave a quick glance over her shoulder and then set her eyes on me.

With knots in my stomach i continued, "Would you like to grab a cup of coffee?" She slightly blushed i think, it was hard to see that detail in the dim streetlight.

"But you already have a coffee," she teased.

i held my coffee cup out at arm's length and poured it out in the gutter. "No i don't."

She smiled with me as she said, "Yes."

We walked down the block into the continuing nightlife that surrounded us. Although it hadn't rained, the street and moonlight glistened on the slick, pitch-black asphalt. As we walked, i interrupted our stroll by asking, "What's your name?" With her soft, sultry voice she said, "Soledad." i was struck by something unexplainable when i heard her say her name. In her silky and lovely tone she proceeded to tell me that her name and the name of the store was pure coincidence. She asked me for my name, i turned to her with a gentle gaze that expressed my joy with her interest. Although, it is out of manners to ask a person their name after they had just asked for yours.

"Juan, but you can call me Johnny," i said even though the only person that called me Johnny was Conor; i believe it was a change done for marketing.

"Juan or Juanito?" she teased.

"Whichever you prefer," i replied. "My mother was the only person to call me Juanito…but so can you." She gave me a playful smirk as we continued our short walk under the street lamps and moon.

As we walked side by side, i was on the outside of the sidewalk, our hands touched. i instantly felt the urge to hold her hand but quickly came to the realization of how strange that would have been. We barely met, but her eyes alone gave me a form of comfort where i wanted to hold her hand for the mere sense of companionship.

We arrived at the little café that stayed open late on the weekends. i held the door open for her, and she smiled in acceptance. Without touching her, like a ghost, i placed my hand in the middle of her back to guide her inside. As she passed me, i received another dose of her perfume that was becoming like heroin to me. i followed her in. We found and sat at a booth by the front window. i ordered a coffee, and she ordered a tea latte. i added some milk to my coffee and sipped it while i sat right in front of her, unable to say a single word. i couldn't say anything, nothing, at least, that wouldn't make me sound like a creep. i sipped my coffee once more and then looked at her. She was waiting there patiently, smiling and stirring her tea.

"You don't talk much do you?" she asked in a friendly yet stern manner. i looked at her in silence.

"What do you do?" she continued.

"i was a writer once upon a time."

"Once upon a time?"

"Yes," i said, sounding rude. i didn't mean to sound that way. It just came out of me like vomit. My inability to function like a human being, or like myself, disgusted me. But it didn't seem to matter; i had grabbed my manhood by asking her out for a cup of coffee, and for some reason, she felt courageous enough to accept my invitation. Nonetheless, i was more intrigued by her essence that i felt back at the bookstore.

"And yourself?" i asked. She finally sipped her tea and then responded.

"I work, and I also write."

My ears perked up like when a deer has heard a sense of danger, but the only danger i found myself in was the danger of becoming so interested in her that i would start to care. i didn't really want to talk about myself. i tried my best to keep her talking without her asking me too many questions about myself, but she wouldn't give up.

"What do you write about?" She asked.

"At the moment, nothing at all."

"Oh c'mon, you must have jotted something down?

"No, no i haven't." i replied and looked down at my steaming cup of coffee.

"Well you said you were a writer, even if it was once upon a time, what did you write?"

"A novel."

She smiled, but it could have been from frustration. "What is your novel about?"

"It's about a man's relentless attempt to find love in a world where love doesn't exist; some said it was about insanity. It's about the similarity between us and used bookstores that are instilled in time, with discovery being only left to chance."

"That's intriguing," she said as she bit her bottom lip. "How did you come up with that idea?"

"i was drunk..." She laughed and covered her mouth as she did so. i bursted out in laughter and felt as if i'd received a cool burst of serotonin in my brain.

"i'm serious," i said through laughs, "i was drunk and didn't get up from my typewriter for two and a half weeks."

i enjoyed her laughter, and although i didn't show it very much, i was feeling neurotic. How can she find so much enjoyment from three very dry words? i found comfort in this, for she didn't take herself all that seriously and apparently had the ability to laugh at anything.

"So you're a hopeful romantic." She said as her laughter eased.

"i'll say i'm a romantic, but i don't say that with great assurance. i also wouldn't say i'm a hopeful romantic; the line between hopeful and desperate is terribly fine." She pondered on what i had said. "For all i know, love could be a figment of our imagination," i drank my coffee as i waited for her response.

"You must believe in love though." i sipped my coffee expectantly. "You speak profoundly. Obviously, you're not married since you invited me out to coffee. You must have love—even for your mother or father, no?" It dawned on me that i didn't know the difference between love and sympathy. My family was gone, was love therefore gone?

"i don't know," i responded.

"You don't know what?"

"If there is love for my parents; it's mainly a form of heartache...they're gone." i sipped my coffee once more.

"Oh, sorry." She reclined in the seat and she had these eyes, sad eyes. "I didn't know; was this recent?"

"No, it's been a few years...it's ok, it doesn't really matter. i can't change it."

"What about a sibling?" she asked trying to fix the conversation.

"i have one."

"Brother or sister?"

"A brother."

"Where is he?"

"i don't know..."

19

She remained quiet and just placed her hand on my forearm. It didn't matter that i was a terrible conversationalist and that even though i did find her beautiful, i was making the best effort to not allow her too close.

"What is your love?" i asked. i could see she was trying to brush off the last conversation.

"Hmm, probably music. I love music; its rhythms, its melodies, everything? What kind of music do you like?" Not only was it a difficult question for anyone to answer but especially nearly impossible for me to answer, nevertheless, i tried.

"i don't really listen to music anymore."

"How's that possible?"

"i don't know." i grew very aware that face to face loquacious intimacy was a weakness of mine. i didn't use the charm i possessed to try to bed her. This was an honest attempt for true human interaction.

"Music can express the emotions we can't explain. True music speaks from the heart directly to another heart. I feel that if everyone listened to music, and listened to their core, that they would hear their own story being told through the vibrations." i raised my cup of coffee to toast; she smiled in acceptance of my agreement.

Years had passed since i even really thought of music and its abilities. i didn't mind not speaking much, if anything, i preferred to just sit there, have a cup of coffee and listen to her soft voice reminding me about love, soul and heartbeats that could be expressed by and for music. Music hadn't been my escape from anything in such a long time. No music was able to move me since the mariachis bid farewell to my mother. i was reminded of that time, not the depressing feelings one endures when a loved one has passed away, but i was reminded how the music was played

20

so lively and lovely while i stood over my mother's grave and drowned in my own tears.

Alas, the night grew old and we had finished our coffee and tea. She said she had to go, and i did as well. i flagged down the waiter and asked for the check. She tried to hand me money.

"What's this for? i asked.

"For my tea."

"No, i insist. i invited you out, so it's my treat."

She accepted, closed her eyes and smiled as if i were to know what that signified, but i gladly took it for what it was. We gathered our coats and headed outside. The night grew chilly, i became aware when she turned to me and her cheeks were rosy. This made her look even lovelier. i didn't say anything regarding her beauty. i was struck by the human condition of never saying anything at the right moment and always having the bravery or the want to say it when it is too late. But i decided to take a chance.

"Where's your car?"

"Oh, I didn't drive."

"Can i walk you home?"

She kindly dismissed my offer and said, "It's okay, thank you, I'm taking the bus."

Without thinking further, i said i'd wait for the bus with her. So we walked the now busy streets filled with drunk and rowdy people and the glistening lights of the city and moon.

We reached the bus stop that ran late on Saturday nights, and we both sat down on the bench. She looked cold, but i dared not make any move that would discomfort her. Yet again, she did take up my invitation for a cup of coffee. She continued to thank me for the night.

"Not at all," said i. "Thank you for accepting the invitation after my first impression; they're only to get worse from here on out."

She laughed, not uncontrollably but enough to cause me to laugh. i felt warm by her laughter and by the stars that shimmered and twinkled in her eyes as she squinted and looked up at the night sky. She placed her hand on my shoulder and pushed me as she laughed. i had the crazy urge to lean in and kiss her, but by the grace of whatever is holy, i gained control.

Beyond the passing nightlife that surrounded us, i heard footsteps that drowned all the others and an essence that interrupted our laughter. It was a humble older gentleman carrying a bucket of red and white roses. He must have been five foot tall and dark. He looked rather quaint with an old Los Angeles Dodgers hat and a thick plaid jacket. He came up to my side of the bench and smiled at me with a tenderness that placed even more wrinkles on his worn face. He spoke to me in Spanish as he realized he had my attention.

*"Romantico, una flor para la dama?"*

i turned and reached into my inside coat pocket. i handed the gentleman whatever bill i had in there.

"Gracias Señor," he said and then handed me a white rose. He must have sensed it was our first time out and decided for himself that a red rose was too much of a flower. He went around me and passed Soledad. i overheard him say, "Es un caballero," to Soledad, and she smiled. As she turned to me, i held out the rose. She laughed as if uncomfortable but accepted my gift. For some egotistical reason, i wanted to know what she thought and what she felt over the flower and my actions, but the last bus of the night was coming to a stop. We both stood up.

"Can i see you tomorrow?" i asked.

22

"What time? I have to go to church."

"Church?" i responded in a state of somewhat shock.

"Yes. Do you go to church?"

"No," i said and placed my head down in shame. i had been raised Catholic but had lost my faith when i started growing up and became more human. i didn't really believe in God, at least, i didn't think so. Up to that point i didn't think i needed too; i had lived my life the way i did regardless if there was a God or not, and i'd probably do the same if given a second chance, but in that moment of shame, came only more questions to my mind. She stood at the first step in the bus facing out towards me, and the impatient bus driver gave me a look of discontent as i held up his route schedule. i felt a wave of emotion for some odd reason. She didn't mention anything else other than attending church the next morning, and that was enough for me to be overwhelmed with the idea of her judging me.

i quickly took out my pocket-sized notebook and wrote down my phone number. i tore the page out and handed it to her. She reached out for it while still holding the rose to her chest and just smiled. She took one more step into the bus and the doors shut. And just like that, the night was over.

i began my walk back home, and in my mind, i played a tune i had never heard before. i walked as if dancing with the cold breeze that tangoed around me. i danced between the lost souls of the Saturday night bars and clubs that were heading the opposite way in this too big of a world of ours. The extra spring in my step was new to me; i'm not entirely convinced i liked it, but i tried to embrace the moment. i tangoed with the breeze in my arms as those drunken heads turned their sorrowful faces away from mine.

i arrived home; i don't recall how late it was, but it must have been late. I turned on the light, and it blinded me for a second as i continued inside for my regular half a liter nightcap. i grabbed a glass, and at my little bar i served up some bourbon and vermouth. i downed the first drink and glanced around my studio.

My eyes locked with the saddened and forgotten eyes of my record player. i walked over to her and dusted off the top of the wooden case. i coughed then placed my glass down. i opened the top and inside was a record i hadn't played in years. i didn't remember owning the particular record. i switched it on and gently placed the needle on the vinyl. She hissed and purred as i played her. i served myself another stiff drink while the Avett Brothers sang and played. My hands strummed with the air to the rhythm, and the ice in my cup swirled around with the melody. Then as the hissing subsided along with the stinging of the whiskey, i remembered the song playing. And when the chorus vibrated throughout my studio, i was struck by the possibility that while we are alive, almost everything matters. i saw the secret paintings and secret colors of my life that i kept to myself, and i felt like bursting into tears. i cut my nightcap short and decided to fall asleep.

i fixed up my futon and rested while watching the moon and stars shine in front of their pitch-black background. i was out for the count. i dreamt a memory of my mother and father. i dreamt of when i was sixteen years old, before my brother passed away. i was deeply infatuated with what i thought was an angel that attended an English class with me. i had finally summed up all the courage that was in my adolescent heart and confessed my love to her. Her name wasn't worth mentioning. It was a Monday afternoon and it was hot. After the final school bell had rung, i stopped her by the parking lot in front of the main office. i remembered thinking that the setting wasn't what one would call romantic, but i found comfort in the idea that my feelings would be enough to make up for this condition. i was wrong. She was as delicate as a flower—at least, that's what i thought at the time; she did let me down just as delicately, but it was a hard thing to go through, especially since my feelings were sincere and as profound as a mother's love.

My brother and i walked all the way home that day, enduring the hot sun and finding relief with the smallest amount of shade the trees had to offer. My brother walked in silence as i walked with a burning pain in my heart that kept reminding me to hold back my tears. When we finally arrived home, my brother stopped me on our porch and, without saying anything or knowing anything about what had happened, held me in his arms. i wept like a small child; my mother must have heard my cries of agony, for she opened the front door.

"Ay mijo, what is wrong?" She had the most heavenly voice. As my brother released me from his hug, i walked to my mother's arms with my head hanging low. For the first time, i felt safe, as if i was back in the womb, and i didn't have to worry about a thing since i was in my mother's protection.

"i told her i loved her," i said in between gasps of air as i drowned in my sea of salty tears.

For as much as i wanted to stop, i couldn't find consolation in anything. i tried working on my schoolwork, watching television and eating my sorrow away with my mother's cooked meals. i sat on our dingy couch with my face in my palms, thinking that this girl finds herself in the arms of another boy. Although i knew i was rejected, i couldn't understand why it hurt so much. My mother told my father who was asleep that afternoon since he worked the graveyard shift at a restaurant. They both sat on the couch with me, one on each side, while my brother watched as he stood leaning against the wall of the hallway.

My father didn't say anything; he just sat there and offered his company while my mother stood up from the couch. i kept my face buried in my hands as my tears ran down my arms and crashed on the canvas of my sneakers. i felt my father's rough hand pat and massage my back as i heard him say, "Oh mijo, look at how you are in the name of love." This only intensified my weeping along with the sounds of the Mariachi music my mother put on the record player. She specifically played the song "Ella" by the great José Alfredo Jimenez. He sang with such a manly yet sincere voice that struck all the melancholic and sympathetic chords in the hearts of all the *machos*.

Very clearly, i heard the sound of glass clinking together along with the sound of liquid being poured. i looked up to see my mother pouring four glasses of *Mezcal*, one for everyone in the room. i felt more Méxicano then than i had ever felt in my young life. This is what men do in our culture: we get our hearts broken, and the only way to heal the broken heart is to drown it with tequila while you cry and sing to *rancheras*. Each drink was to be toasted in her name. i cried even more as i accepted the loss forever. Each sip of mezcal burned my throat; its burn made me realize that there was a reason all these Mexican troubadours sang about heartbreak and loneliness...because of beautiful women like the one who broke my heart. Those women are unwilling to love, but most importantly, they're unwilling to be loved.

~~~~~

The knives of light hit my eyelids; i opened them to the start of a new day. Sunday; i hated Sundays. It's not because it's the Lord's Day, not in particular, but mainly because my days and nights were haunted by the wistful harmony of Billie Holiday's voice on every gloomy Sunday. The day was gray like the color of a dog and unusually humid for this California town. i sat on my bed, placed my feet on the cold ground and lit a cigarette as i contemplated, only for a moment, the night before.

Naturally my mind wandered back to the memory of my father and mother. i hadn't dreamt of my father for what seemed to be another lifetime. How i missed him as well, unfortunately, i only had memories of him—not a photograph or any form of material he had once possessed. With everything in our society pointing to the contrary, even a single memory of a person is all you'll need in this life. Material can be seized or burned in a fire, but a memory will follow you to the funeral parlor.

He was of mid stature, dark and handsome like a bottle of bourbon. He wore his sun worn face and neck everywhere he went. He was a man of few words, so his experiences were often left to our imaginations and terrible inabilities to guess. He always sat in silence at the dinner table and would often look at our mother and us with his very tender eyes, as if he was incapable of any form of verbal expression. He was born in *Tijuana,* i think. Or in some *pueblo* my brother and i were never able to visit. He wasn't an angry or bitter person; he was content with the little bit that we had, and that was all right with me. He was weathered by his childhood under the hot sun as a migrant worker in the fields of Oxnard. The beatings from the flaming sun were apparent in his rugged yet youthful face. Although my grandfather used him as a heavy bag as a boy, he never laid a finger on us. He often resorted to asking us why we had done what we had done and let us feel the guilt from his disappointment. He and my mother raised us in the unconventional way of unconditional love and the occasional raised voice.

He couldn't read or write, but somehow i had fallen in love with that feature. He was a simple man, and i wished i could become half of that. He taught me that luxury isn't essential for happiness, but elegance can be worn on the sleeve of any man regardless of rich or poor. He had gone to México that summer following my first heartbreak to attend his mother's funeral, and the day he was to cross the deserts to come back to us, we never heard from him again.

With this in mind, i finished my cigarette and decided to get dressed to enjoy a cup of coffee out on the town. It was around one o'clock in the afternoon, and i was of the belief that i was enjoying an early start to the day in the week i disliked the most. i stepped out the front door of my studio apartment building and was greeted by the fresh breeze of a cool afternoon. i smoked another cigarette as i walked a few blocks to a little café that probably only sat fifteen people at the most. i ordered a coffee with milk and a croissant. i sat by the small bay window by the front door and watched the people out and about; everyone passed one another through the beautiful fruit and fresh meats being offered by the farmers' market that took place every Sunday.

i thought of Soledad and searched every passing face for hers. The coffee stung my belly and the croissant did little to help. i knew i wouldn't see nor find Soledad at that moment, but my nerves were restless. i had hoped to casually find her again just like the night before, but this hope was held onto for only a brief moment.

After a humble breakfast, i decided to head a bit further downtown towards the Cathedral. There was a little park that was like the poor man's Central Park of New York minus the heinous crimes and muggings. Upon arriving at the park, i was greeted by a very lovely, older Mexican woman selling churros and *elotes* with cream and cheese on a stick. i bought a churro and sat next to her on a bench that was next to her little stand. She began talking to me about how she just got to the country and had to support her two children and a couple of grandchildren that remained in México with their mother. i was saddened yet smiled at her story for it reminded me of my parents. Just then, the pigeons started flying wildly all around the park, filling the sky as the Cathedral bells struck. i couldn't remember if that meant church was about to begin or if it called for the end of mass.

The sounds of the park with the vendors and the crowd that was exiting the church had become alive. i lit a cigarette as my eyes consumed the rustle and bustle from all the people dressed in their Sunday Best. The skies opened up and a beam of light laid its ethereal touch on one single person that i viewed exiting through the Cathedral doors and onto its front steps. It was Soledad. She seemed to be accompanied by who i assumed to be her mother. i stood up and bid farewell to the Mexican woman and headed to see if i could sum up the courage to greet Soledad once more.

i approached her and got nervous, mainly because i felt like i was a stalker, but this feeling was masked and overcome when i knew i wanted to see her again. As i got closer, i puffed my cigarette as i looked up at her standing at the top of the marble steps. i put out my cigarette out of respect for the church and slowly made my way up the stairs. Her back was to me, so i was sure i'd unfortunately greet her by surprise. The older lady she was talking too looked at me dead in the eyes and smiled as if she knew who i was. Right then i gently placed my hand on Soledad's right shoulder.

She turned around, smiled and looked around in what i expected to be a look of surprise.

"Juanito," she beamed. Her voice sent a lightning bolt and shivers down my back and wobbled my knees.

"Soledad," i said in almost a whisper as i gathered as much of a breath as i could. As she completely turned to greet me, i held out my hand. Her soft and silky fingers wrapped around mine. Without a word, i raised her hand as she gently smiled; i kissed the back of her hand. She seemed once more taken back by my actions and blushed as if my breath on her already warm hand was suffused with the fire that burned in my chest.

She seemed anxious with our encounter; i noticed her racing speech and the back and forth looks between the older lady and i. She placed her hand on my forearm and looked back at the woman.

"Mom, this is Juanito…or Johnny."

"Good afternoon, Señora," i said as i stuck out my hand. Silently she reached out and shook my hand. In an effort to be viewed as a gentleman, i raised her hand to my lips with a little bit of resistance from her but kissed it nonetheless. The air grew silent; her mother scarcely blinked, her eyes burning with little enthusiasm, more like a lioness in the process of protecting her cub.

The silence was broken by Soledad asking if i had attended mass. As if that were the only way to be able to run into her so randomly.

"No," i replied.

"You don't belong to any church?" Her mother had finally broken her bout with silence. i looked at Soledad and then set my eyes on her mother.

"Not at the moment."

i felt Soledad's blush and downcast eyes as i realized i shouldn't be saying such a thing to her mother. i attempted to please her mother. "i was actually baptized at this Cathedral. i came to hear the sermon, but unfortunately, i showed up an hour too late."

She wasn't convinced, and i didn't blame her. The fact that i didn't blame her made her hold it against me even more. Her eyes alone yelled at me, "You're a liar!"

i turned to Soledad, whose radiant aura shot out of the ends of her hair and surrounded her face and eyes. Once more i felt like i did in the bookstore, mesmerized, yet still possessed by the shadows that remained deep in my core. Although i didn't know her at all really, her aura of friendliness and sincerity was apparent and did nothing to make me turn the other way and be haunted by another journey of regret.

"May i see you later?"

"Maybe," she demurred.

i smiled, "Maybe...at the coffee shop on the corner of Fourth and main?"

"What time?" She looked at her mother who in turn just stared back at her.

"Seven?"

"Alright. I'll see you there." They left; i watched them both, mainly Soledad, as they made their way down the Cathedral steps and onto the rowdy streets.

The aroma of churros and other fried goods crowded the street. "i have another date," i crooned to myself, and yet i was overcome by the feeling of laziness, perhaps, where i felt convinced that i actually didn't want to go out later that night. i had become used to not having anyone to share my evenings with and part of me didn't want to start.

~~~~~

i walked back home. i lit a cigarette as i entered my apartment and looked at my typewriter on my desk, glowing as the light pierced my window and brightened the surface of the desk while the rest of the room was cursed with darkness. i inhaled deeply and let out the smoke from my nostrils and walked over to sit at my desk. i held the cigarette between my chapped lips as i loaded a blank piece of newsprint paper into my typewriter and braced my hands above the keys. My cell phone rang; the smoke stung my eyes as i reached for my phone. It was Conor.

"Hello?"

"Johnny, it's me."

"i know, what's up?"

"Just checking up on you and to see how your synopsis is coming along?"

"It's only been two days or so since we spoke. i'm typing something up as we speak." He let out a breath of air.

"That's great Johnny, I actually need something from you in two weeks." i didn't say anything, i couldn't.

"My boss is breathing down my neck and I need your help," he said as i cleared my throat. "Tell me you understand."

After a few seconds i responded, "i understand."

The volcano inside me was perturbed. A deep rumbling was happening in my core and my head filled with smoke. i stared at the blank page and knew i was doomed. i put my cigarette out on the blank page that haunted my typewriter.

The next few hours consisted of countless cigarettes and a pint of whiskey while listening to slow jazz on my record player as my eyes became teary over a blank piece of paper that had ashes and a burnt hole in the middle of it. "It is the business aspect of the literary world," i told myself. i thought of Soledad and wished she were in my apartment with me. She was an aspiring writer, and the only thing i would be able to say or do is pay her my condolences. i hadn't read any of her writings or poetry and part of me didn't really want to. Not because i didn't think she'd be a great writer but because fiction tells the truth through lying, and i was afraid of what i would find out, not only about her, but i was afraid of what i might find out about myself.

Hours passed and the sky grew darker with its decorative stars to set a mood that i couldn't explain. It was 6:30pm and not a single word had been punched onto a single piece of paper. Needless to say, i gave up on the idea of trying to write and needed to mentally prepare to meet Soledad once again. i fixed myself a quick sandwich; i hadn't eaten since i ate the churro earlier that day. i wasn't all that hungry, but i ate a sandwich along with a glass of water and headed out the door.

i stepped foot on the street in front of my building and was struck by the sunset. Vibrant oranges and pinks spread out across the sky like wings of an eagle; gray and blue clouds flitted with the vibrant colors that reflected off the windows of the tallest buildings in town. Everyone on the street just kept walking, undeterred from their boring routines. For a second i felt like a young boy; a rain struck my heart like when one loves in vain; i felt my brother's presence right there and then. He would have loved this sight, if anything he probably gets a better view wherever he finds himself. i stood there only for a few moments; i didn't want to keep Soledad waiting, much less waiting for me. i walked into the sun and its painted sky with only my shadow chasing my silhouette and the whole strange world in front of me. Like it always is, for a ramblin' hobo on the road.

i walked against the crowds in a familiar fashion as i made my way to the café where i was to meet with Soledad. i ran into a familiar face upon arriving to the café around the corner. It was the older gentleman from the night before, from whom i had bought the rose for Soledad. He greeted me with all smiles as if we were longtime friends. He ignored the rest of the people who, in turn, ignored him and he walked right up to me in his struggling gait.

"Good evening, Señor," he said with a friendly grin and asked, "Some flowers for your friend?"

i offered my hand to him. He took it without hesitation; his hands were rough and dry. Not that it mattered, but i took it as a sign of hard work. He pulled his white bucket around to his front side as it hung from the old, greasy rope from his shoulder. He had some nice flowers, the basic roses in both white and red being sold as singles. But he had other flowers that flirted and teased my eyes. i touched the small and white petals that were as soft as clouds and as gentle as love itself. My fingertips danced along the wavy petals that flowed in between each other. It was the only bunch and there must have been more than a dozen flowers in the bunch.

"Mini white carnations" he said in English with an accent that was similar to my mother's.

"Cuanto?" i asked.

"For you my friend, five dollars."

It was really inexpensive, and that made me feel bad. He seemed like he was an honest man, and judging by the full bucket of flowers, he must be desperate to sell at least one. i reached for my wallet that was inside my inner coat pocket as he grabbed the bunch of mini carnations. i paid him.

"Don't be late to see her, Señor," he said. i silently nodded my thanks and went on my way.

i arrived at the café where i was to meet Soledad again. It was five till' seven. i lit a cigarette as i waited. Soledad was a block and a half away when i spotted her. She hadn't seen me waiting, so i very passively placed the white mini carnations behind my back with my right hand and smoked my cigarette with my left. She finally got closer and brightened up the black evening with her smile. Her eyes followed my hand as i moved my cigarette from my side and up to my lips; i knew she didn't like me smoking, or smoking in general, yet she never said anything about it. Even i disliked how i always smelled like an ashtray, but i couldn't break the habit.

As she reached me, smoke came out of my nostrils, and i stomped out my cigarette. Before she was able to say a word, i swung my hand around and greeted her chest with the mini carnations. Again she didn't say anything, but she seemed to gladly accept them; this i knew because of her subtle laughter. She had beautiful teeth as well. i found it odd that i noticed such a thing but displaced the thought as i realized i had become smitten. i invited her into the café as if it were my home; i held open the door and then followed her in. i invited her for coffee or tea again. She ordered her tea, and i ordered a coffee, and we were able to find an open couch in front of a fireplace that was burning.

She looked lovely as always and cozy as well. She was wearing an olive green ribbon in her hair that paired with her wool green coat. Jeans and a pair of nice leather boots, she looked elegant—more so than how i saw her earlier in front of the Cathedral. She sipped her tea as we sat there in silence. i wasn't really in the mood for conversation, but she was somehow capable of getting poetic prose rolling in my mind. She said she brought some

35

of her writings. i thought to myself, "i'd be honored," but decided best not to be so obsequious. i nodded slightly and raised an eyebrow in encouragement.

From her bag came out a notebook that flaunted printed images of painted flowers and a pink lace ribbon tying it shut. She handed it to me, and without hesitation, i opened the notebook and began to read the first page. She had filled at least half or more than half of the notebook with poetry and prose. She sat in silence and kind of seemed to daydream as she glowed a golden red while the fireplace flames danced in her clear eyes. i remember actually liking what she wrote, and that shocked me, considering my natural state of pessimism.

i got lost in her writings; the words were like melancholy hymns or melodies. They told such a sad story. i felt she was heartbroken like i was; she probably had to endure the conventional heartbreak along with what i had to endure. What i endured was more like being born with a broken heart; no one really had broken it; it was just broken to begin with. But i felt something else through her writings. i got to get to know her a bit; within all the heartbreak, she always seemed able to find something to be grateful for. This conflicted me. She was so filled with hope and optimism, and i was filled with despair and doubt. i was a minor chord, and she was a major chord; i was poetry, and she was prose.

i used to have these conversations with my brother where we were able to converse about books, poetry and music without uttering a word. No one else until that day spoke our secret language—no one until Soledad. The words flowed from page to page like fine wine as the flames from the fireplace grew brighter and hotter.

Even though it was only our second time spending time together, she asked if i was interested in collaborating with her. i asked her what she would like to write, for i had been having difficulty writing recently.

"A poem," she said.

A strong sense of intimidation churned inside me. i couldn't write a single word as I attempted to write fiction, and there we were about to try to write a poem. i loved writing poetry, however, it was never an easy thing to write. Poetry is able to talk about the most difficult things in life in an easy and intimate fashion. i wasn't sure i was ready for her to be that familiar with me, but i agreed to try and write a poem with her.

We ordered some more coffee and tea and then she turned to me, "You start the poem."

"About what?"

"I don't know, you're the writer, what do you want to express?" her lips turned up in a shy smile.

"i'm not all that sure to be honest."

She sat in silence.

For the life of me, i couldn't write anything. My frustration must have been apparent, for she placed her hand on my forearm and said gently, "Write from here," pointing to her heart, "and then here," lightly touching her temple.

"It's not that easy…at least not for me." She then reached for her notebook, and i caught her hand midway. "Wait," i said, "i think i have something." She smiled and leaned back in the couch. i began writing something, "if love was a handwritten letter…" i was in shock by the time my hand and pen had lifted off the notebook. The page was no longer blank.

i quickly read what i had written and then picked up the notebook in such a way to be able to hold onto it and point to what i had written. Something fell out from between the pages. Without glancing at her, i went to pick it up. It was a white, semi-dried rose. My rose, the rose i had given her the night before. i picked it up.

She blushed and said, "I wanted to keep it."

Once more, the coward that is in everyman consumed the words i could have said when one is flattered by a pretty girl. i held onto the rose dearly as i flipped through the pages of her notebook and placed it back. i held the rose as if it were my heart that she kept in between her deepest thoughts and secrets.

Not long after that, she announced she had better get going. One has no choice but to respect the decision of a lady. We finished our hot drinks and went towards the door. i wanted so badly at the very least to hold her hand, but i noticed she grew hesitant to even look at me in the eye. We chatted very poorly as we strolled to the bus stop. Unfortunately for me, the bus arrived as we arrived.

She gave me a quick hug goodbye, and that was the end of the night. i lit a cigarette and began to walk home.

Something came over me. Childlike, i wanted to break out in dance, tears and laughter to a song, like a mediocre pop song i barely knew, like the fall and it's morning dew. i wanted to get lost just to be able to find her again. It was innocent but profound, like a grammar school love. i was able to make her laugh and with that came longing. Not a sexual longing, but like a child, i wanted her every time she laughed and smiled. i wanted to explore every corner of her mind and every flower in her heart. i barely knew her, she barely knew me, and yet i found myself in love. Of course not with her, i didn't know her quite enough, nor her i. But i knew the moment i had read her writings i fell in love, maybe not with her but with her essence, which is stronger than loving just the person. And this gave me something. Hope, perhaps not hope for her and i, but hope for humanity and its future.

i arrived home, had a smoke, and opened up a bottle of wine i had been saving for a special occasion. i walked over to my record player and played some *Chicano* oldies. i drank my wine like a first timer, fast, as if it were water. i smoked my cigarettes and hummed along with *Thee Midniters* as we both agreed on how the towns we lived in were lonely.

Although i sang along, at the moment i didn't exactly agree to the fullest. One has to embrace their solitude. i never once believed that my solitude was the cause of all the negativity in my life. Due to current events, i had become aware of all the positive things and how they were made possible by my ability to thrive in my solitude. Being a writer is a lonely life, but there is not another way. i never have been bothered to run into the late Friday and Saturday nights and act along with the stupidity that goes on in nightclubs. They aren't exactly like bars or coffee shops. Those places are different, some of the people who go out to coffee shops or even bars for that matter, can often spend more than two minutes with a book and not get bored. Perhaps i hadn't tried all that hard, but i had never been impressed with someone i had met at a club. Even if i got laid, i was never all that interested. But a night of loneliness was thrown out and replaced with an awkward morning and plenty of booze to drink to forget.

i wasn't really interested in many things. My heart could be invested in many things, but naturally i either outgrew or i simply didn't care for common tasks. My heart laments from our human condition. i often get embarrassed by being part of the human species, but my loyal and noble heart makes me stand next to my fellow humans, even though they are often embarrassing themselves with thoughts and actions of self-entitlement and a "me against the world" attitude. i wished not to compare my feelings to those of Jesus, but despite all my efforts to remain and live a life in solitude, my heart has always been heavy. Not heavy by weight of anger or guilt, but heavy with love and compassion.

i laid out my futon, dragged my cigarette one more time and laid my head back on the pillow. My eyelids grew heavy and the light no longer bothered my brain. i fell into a deep sleep.

~~~~~

i awoke to the sound of my cell phone ringing. i went to the kitchen and drank the few drops of wine that were left in the bottle from the night before to aid my headache. It was Soledad who called but i didn't answer on time. i tried to call her back but was greeted by her voicemail. i was about to hang up, and then i heard her voice on the "leave a message" message. Her voice was as sweet and golden as thick honey. i kept listening to her until i heard the beep, then i hung up without a word.

As i hung up, my phone gave me the notice of an unheard voicemail. Her voice shot a bolt of lust and desire down my back.

"Juanito, its Soledad calling you. I wanted to see if you'd join me for an early lunch at ten o'clock? I'll be at *La Rose Blanc;* I hope to see you…"

i lit a cigarette and took a puff before i placed it in the ashtray. i got ready in a somewhat lazy fashion, but it was the best i could do. i walked out of my building with my cigarette between my lips and looked around the street. My natural melancholy feelings took over as i watched the passing people. i tried to shake off my feelings for i was to see Soledad, and dared to say, ever since meeting Soledad, my views had been challenged as they often are by your parents when they try to talk some sense into you as a teenager.

40

i kept walking to the little French style café. "i should have gotten flowers," i thought as i reached the front steps of the café. i took two steps back from the door until i noticed Soledad sitting in a booth big enough for two by the front window. The flamboyancy of the flowers that were sitting along the windowsill was overpowered by the aroma of coffee and baked bread. She looked beautiful as she always did. Dressed rather elegantly for a meeting with me. She didn't notice me as i stood there for a brief moment. i walked towards the smell of the baked bread, coffee and the white roses that combined, served as a stimulant of some sort. i felt manic. Quickly, i walked towards the windowsill and plucked a few white, soft roses for Soledad. i walked inside.

The aroma was warm and inviting; an angelic light that was from a smile blinded me. She spotted me as i walked in. She smiled a tad bit more as she took notice of the roses in my hand; they were soft, but the thorns dug into my palm. As i walked to the booth, i noticed that she was wearing a vintage white dress, and her hair was done in a wavy fashion that took me back to the 1940's. She was cute, her and her cat eye sunglasses that were on the tabletop next to her clasped hands. i handed her the roses, and she laughed. This excited me but not exactly in a sexual way; i couldn't make sense of it.

She started talking. Every time she talked, i felt warmth suffuse my chest. The heat intensified every time i got her to laugh and her cheeks would wrinkle and turn a deep red. Her laughter gave me a burst of serotonin; i felt a cooling in the nerves of my brain; she made me smile, highly neurotic. i felt drunk. i only drank for the ability to feel love in one way or another.

Being a natural depressive, one tends to feel things very profoundly. Every time i was in the presence of

Soledad, with every cup of coffee shared and every rose given the death sentence in her name, felt like my purgatory. Women really are beautiful creatures; even a generic smile on their behalf and every curve that they offer. i was reminded of how we humans have a condition where we can have beautiful yet sad memories or ideals. Like when Soledad smiled and her laughter would fill the room without fearing judgment, i thought of things that i could take to the grave and how her essence would be one of those cherished things. i would love to be buried with a photograph of Soledad. Not in an obsessive manner but in the way that i wouldn't forget her face, and so i wouldn't be afraid when i'd be six feet under, to feel that i can possess her charm and essence and to feel alive. i hope others see this as a loving ideation and not a dark obsession. i have yet to kiss her. i've held her hand in order to kiss the backside of her hand but never held it with the intentions of walking down the avenue. The conversations i have had with her i wish not to mention, selfishly, i want to keep them only for myself. Some things are worth sharing, and some things are worth keeping to one's self, even though it could be a cherished memory that challenged one's virtue and values.

When i met Soledad at the French café i admired the way she presented herself and her natural beauty in a shy manner. i didn't speak much and she took notice but didn't mention my silence; we just enjoyed each other's presence for a moment until she decided to break the silence.

"Thank you again for the flowers, Juanito. The roses are beautiful."

"i plucked them myself."

"Do you like flowers Juanito?"

"i thought you might like them." She just stared into my eyes. They were so easy to look at but so difficult to read. "i never really thought of whether i liked flowers or not, i just thought you would appreciate receiving them," i said and then added, "If you allow me, i'd like to continue to annoy the shit out of you with more flowers." Her eyes lit up and got glossy as she held in a laugh. i wanted to kiss her right then and there, but again i was able to take control of these impulses. Although, i didn't understand why i felt the need to control my desires; i assumed it was out of fear. Rejection was the first thing that came to my troubled mind, but this thought i had tried to place to rest. It was my belief that one should not fear rejection, for there would always be something better waiting ahead. This thought also brought me lots of comfort, for i believed, or liked to believe, that i was more optimistic than an observer would give me credit. Although, i was a night owl, i always loved the idea of days under the sun like when i was a boy, and the red and golden beams of light would enter through my bedroom windows. That's when i knew my mother was right; no matter how dark the night may be, it is only a matter of time before you have something new to appreciate.

We finished our hot drinks. i gathered myself while she grabbed her cat eye sunglasses and white roses that glowed radiantly as they were struck by the sunlight through the café window. We exited onto the street that had a good amount of people walking around; we joined them in silence as Soledad obscured herself by placing on her sunglasses that made her look mysterious and enthralling.

"What to do now?" She asked.

i shrugged my shoulders, "Do you have anything to do? Are you free the rest of the afternoon?"

"Yes," she said as she looked at me. i looked deep into the darkness of her sunglasses but knew that the prettiest clear hazel eyes were looking back at mine. Having asked two questions, i had no idea which of the two she had answered.

i looked down at our feet as we strolled down the avenue. As we strolled, our hands had bumped into one another. i decided that it didn't really matter whether or not i tried to hold her hand. i had nothing to fear and nothing to lose. Our hands bumped once more, and this time i reached to free her right hand of the roses i had given her, and i held them in my right hand. She looked at me with curiosity but allowed me to take charge. i held her roses and held her hand with my left hand. She beamed as we continued down the avenue. By holding her hand, i felt, i knew that i was the richest man walking down the street.

Still holding my hand, she stopped and turned to me. "Seriously what can we do?"

"i don't know," i said blankly.

"Let's do something spontaneous," she said. The pervert in me thought she meant sex, but this thought died a quick death as she took off her sunglasses to get a better read of me. She squinted as the February sun glistened in her clear eyes. i didn't respond. She perked up, "Let's go to the beach."

"Really?"

"It's rather warm for a February. Haven't you ever wanted to just *do something*? Sometimes you just have to do it and not think about it."

Taking her sage advice, i wrapped one arm around her waist and placed my other hand gently upon her cheek. She blushed, and i felt the warmth of her rosy cheeks in the palm of my hand as i pressed my lips upon hers. i felt the coarse texture of her white cotton dress that had a silk ribbon wrapped around her waist. i pulled away and then gave her another peck as her eyes remained closed. She gave a smile bigger than this world of ours, then she opened her eyes.    "Yes," i agreed, "let's go to the beach."

We hopped on an express train that would take us from downtown San Jose into the downtown boulevards of Santa Cruz. She took a nap on the train as she rested her head on my shoulder. She was closer to the window, but i stared at the woods as we passed through the mountains. i didn't really want to go out of town. i felt great when i finally kissed Soledad, but i started getting depressed. i couldn't explain it, and i will never be able too.

The good thing is they have a full bar on the lounge car. i tried not to wake or disturb Soledad as she napped peacefully. She barely moved when i slipped my shoulder from beneath her head, her hair smelling of spring blossoms. She rested her head against the seat as she faintly moaned. i stood up and gently stroked her hair as i watched her sleep. She looked so…innocent, not that she wasn't innocent, but like Tom Waits once said in a lyric, "You're innocent when you dream." As i stood there watching and listening to Soledad take her deep breaths, i could see her chest and back expand with each inhale. A form of sadness ached my heart once more; i felt a warmth in my chest along with my face flush. It was a lovely sadness, like when one hears a beautiful woman tell her sad story. This too was like my purgatory, spending time with someone, especially a beautiful woman. Women really are something else; their smiles and secrets are enough to turn kings into beggars. i, too, am a victim to such effects. Although i avoided many encounters, even if they were proven to be friendly, i had a weakness to never being able to say "no." But this was different, with Soledad, i felt i didn't need to pretend to be something i was not; as she slept, she was so lovely, and i was depressive; she was so innocent, and i was a literary fraud; i smoked, and she didn't. i wanted to sit there again with her head resting on my shoulder and just embrace, not only her, but also the moment in a way that was so innocent i felt no other grown mortal could understand.

i left Soledad and made my way to the lounge car, passing strangers with the same destination but in an alternate realm from the small universe i inhabited with Soledad at that moment. i walked and was overwhelmed with the sound of the train speeding on the tracks as i passed through each cabin door. i stopped between one of the cars and just absorbed the sound of the wheels turning on the steel alloy tracks. i pretended that i was hopping the train to nowhere in particular, and that i was on an adventure of a lifetime. The moment passed, and i entered the next car; it was the lounge car. It was completely different compared to the other coach cars that held all the passengers. The car was dimly lit and smelled of fresh cut limes and liquor. Along the walls of the car was a single blue, white and green neon tube light that reminded me of a bar in Reno or something. The car was empty with only the bartender standing behind the bar with his arms crossed. He was a young man, maybe around my age, wearing a black button up shirt under a cheap blazer that i'm sure was provided for him. i walked up to the bar.

"What are you having?" he asked without moving, although he wasn't rude for he offered somewhat of a smile.

"A Manhattan, on the rocks."

"What kind of bourbon?"

"Four Roses Single Barrel if you have it."

He nodded in compliance. He grabbed a bourbon glass and dunked it in ice, poured some vermouth in it, swirled it around and filled the rest with the rich, amber liquor from an unopened bottle, the roses embossed in the heavy glass reminding me ashamedly of Soledad's roses. He threw the final touch of the cherry in it and then slid it my way. i picked up the glass before it had completely stopped on the bar counter, and i gulped it down. i wiped my lips to ease the stinging from the ice and picked the cherry from the glass and ate it. He looked at me in what i assumed was disgust; i felt his judgment burn in his blue eyes that paired well with his surfer blonde hair, greased back with a strong fragranced pomade.

"Let me have another, this time in a big boy glass."

He just stared at me; i almost laughed at the whole situation he was trying to create but instead just leaned over the counter. i looked around and grabbed an upside down pint glass that was next to the collection of nearly full bottles of liquor. i placed the glass on the bar and looked at him, "This one will do, thank you."

He grabbed it, filled it halfway with ice and mixed the drink then topped it with a cherry and, like Sam Malone, once again slid the glass across the counter top.

"Can i have a bottle of water as well?" He obliged me. i paid the tab, tipped him and left the lounge car still holding my extra-large Manhattan.

i must have drunk the drink too fast, or i exited the lounge from the wrong door because it seemed that i had gotten lost. None of the faces, although they were from painted strangers, were familiar to me at all. But i kept pushing through the doors with a bottle of water in one hand and a big glass of bourbon in the other. The sound of the train on the tracks intensified the anxiety that grew in me. i was sure Soledad still napped, but i was worried she might wake before i returned. In a funny way, i wanted to see her as she napped once more. It was something else, it was like the feeling of watching a child sleep, and it was so peaceful and warm. It can't be achieved any other way.

i kept going through the doors, going through the doors, and going through the doors until i was finally stopped in my tracks. Blinded by rays of sunlight that peeked through the redwoods that we passed at an incredible speed. Yet, time seemed to slow down. i felt my thoughts grow numb by the sight. "What a beauty," i thought. i wondered if this was what death would be like. Everyone speaks ill of death, but i beg to differ. Death, yes, can be sad for everyone but full of light for the one who passes. i'm sure there are marvelous redwood trees in death, or maybe we become them. But this sight, i felt like it had been here waiting for me all along. No one else was here to view or absorb this at all. It was as if it were only for my eyes. i didn't even think of Soledad at that moment; i only looked at the red and golden sunlight that was carrying a collection of sad memories through the wind. i felt pathetic and nostalgic at the same time. i wanted to burst into tears or for Soledad to hold me in silence there in the sunlight. The room was on the upper level so there weren't any obstructions of the view; it was mainly all glass, and the seats were situated down the middle of the cabin. i sat down, gulped my Manhattan, and shut my eyes as i let the beams of light carry every bit of their humanity that they could offer to me and burn my skin. It's moments or places like these in which i wished i could spend my final hours. To slowly die as a growing beauty continues its lavish of affection.

Depression has a way of making you a romantic, an irrational romantic—to feel everything and nothing at the same time.

i gulped down the rest of my drink, ate the cherry and placed the glass on the seat next to me. i got up, gave one last glance at the view and then exited the empty car. i found the car where Soledad and i were seated and was pleasantly surprised to have found Soledad still asleep. i ran my hand through her hair gently in hopes to not wake her and then placed my lips and kiss upon her brow. i gently raised her head and sat down and slipped my shoulder beneath her head. She groaned a bit as she dug her head into my chest and started to wake up.

She yawned a cute yawn and i kissed her. She kissed me back, and after she smiled and laughed, i kissed her again.

"How was your slumber?"

"Good, thank you," she said as she stretched out her body. i wrapped my arms around her, and she once again placed her head on my shoulder. She looked even prettier when she barely woke up. This wasn't the first time i had been with a woman when she had just awakened; those times were often after a one-night stand. i never gave much thought on how it would feel to see and interact with a girl right after she had woken up. And i have to say, now, there is nothing like it.

"Are we there yet?"

"We should be arriving soon." i patted her head. She seemed to like that as far as i could tell, for she purred like a cat as i did so.

The train was making its decline of the Santa Cruz Mountains down to the downtown area and the beaches. We wouldn't be too far from the boardwalk. A voice on the intercom announced our arrival to the station and we prepared to hop off the train.

We exited to the rustle and bustle of downtown Santa Cruz. People were everywhere despite it being a cool and chilly February afternoon along the coast. Soledad grabbed my hand as we walked down the boulevard with the giant Santa Cruz Beach Boardwalk on the horizon. We stopped along the way and browsed the little mom and pop shops that were all over the place. i mainly just watched and enjoyed watching Soledad browse the places for vintage things. We would exchange laughter and smiles as she tried on different sunglasses; some sensual, some casual and some just simply outrageous.

We kept walking and reached another shop that had hats for both men and women for sale, and she placed on my head a grey wool paperboy cap i actually really liked. She tried on a white wide brim sun hat that fit her personality more than charm itself. As she looked at herself in the mirror, i just tried to understand what i was feeling. Again, i was at a loss of words. A few days ago i was ready to leave this world, and she and i were complete strangers. i bought the paperboy hat she had picked for me, and i attempted to buy the white wide brim sun hat she was wearing, but she didn't let me. i understood why; i wouldn't want someone i barely knew buying me something even if it was inexpensive. She bought her own hat and we went on our way.

i lit a cigarette as we continued to walk and asked, "Did you want to go to a beach or the boardwalk maybe?"

"Let's walk on the boardwalk. I... I don't really like the sand."

i laughed. "You don't like the sand? But you wanted to come to the beach?"

She laughed and explained, "I don't mind walking on the beach, but wet sand everywhere bugs me."

i kept smoking and just smiled. As the boardwalk grew bigger as we got closer, it went from being a spec into its own metropolis; with the screams coming from the roller coaster rides, it was the musical metropolis of the area. As we approached, the salty sea breeze flooded the air that filled our lungs.

Previously, whenever i was with a woman (mainly having a drink with a girl at a bar), i found myself never really all that interested, but i would always stroke their thighs and egos by telling them how beautiful they were, again, a trait of mine when i'm in that purgatory. Only this time, i felt that i was, in fact, interested—interested to know the most innocent things about Soledad. She hadn't opened up about herself, so i assumed others had never really asked. i took a drag from my cigarette and grazed her shoulder with a light finger; her skin was warm from the sun and soft as a silk sheet. She turned to me.

"What's your favorite color?"

"What?" she laughed, "why?"

"i want to know…"

Her attention turned back to the direction we were walking. "It sort of changes."

"Like with the seasons?" i got her to laugh again. Damn i loved it when she laughed.

"Blue. My favorite color is blue." She looked back at me. "What's your favorite color?"

The first thing i thought of was the fact that she returned the question. It wasn't so much how i would answer the question but the fact that she asked it in return. To me that meant she genuinely cared what my favorite color was.

"i never really thought about it," i exhaled cigarette smoke.

"You must have a favorite color. Everyone has one, don't they?"

The truth was it didn't really matter. Not to me, having a favorite color was for children. And i hadn't been a child for a long time. i had stopped being a child the day my brother was buried, and i became a grown man shortly thereafter when my mother passed away. But at that moment, i became aware of the simplicity of thinking, and the simplicity of life, and the simplicity of having a favorite color. i'm sure my brother, mother and father all had a favorite color, but unfortunately, i was too occupied with the selfish behavior of taking them for granted to have had asked them such a simple question. i looked at Soledad.

"Mine's blue as well."

"Why blue?" she asked, and i took a deep inhale of the cigarette that acted a lot like a pacifier in times like those.

Again, the truth was because the color blue would now forever remind me of Soledad. Forevermore, when i remembered Soledad, i would remember: the sea, the spring, the sky, but most of all, the sun and the flames that would forever burn for her. Her memory would lead me to the profound meanings of untold stories and the most obscure substances of art and poetry.

"i don't know," i lied and let out a big puff of smoke.

"You must know."

"Why do you like the color blue then?" i teased.

She didn't respond, perhaps it was because she had another profound reason she couldn't tell me. Or maybe she didn't really know why that was her favorite color. Either way, i placed the cigarette between my lips and grabbed her by the hand as we reached the steps to the boardwalk entrance.

"Let's just look around," she said, and i agreed. i stomped off my cigarette and we entered the boardwalk, surprisingly busy for a chilly day. Nonetheless, people were out, and the surfers that looked like a pod of seals were out enjoying the waves that the cold California coast had to offer.

The sounds of the boardwalk were musical. Bumper cars crashing and the young and old screams coming from the giant roller coasters and swinging pirate ships. The sounds of talking and laughter also filled the atmosphere, but it was the voice of Soledad that would cut through the most to me. The crowds dispersed a bit as we walked further onto the pier. i lit another cigarette until Soledad looked at me and said, "Let's ride the gondola."

We entered a blue tram that was just big enough for two adults or three small children. She sat to the outside of the tram, so she had the view looking out to the sea, but it didn't bother me. She was my view and that was all that mattered to me for that moment in time. We held hands for a little while until she pulled my arm around her and rested her head on my chest as she looked out towards the sea. The waves crashed in the not so distant horizon and within me there was a colorful blooming reef, full of life and light. i was afraid for what that meant, and i was terrified. The sun moved over the rise as the gondola came to a stop, and our ride was over.

"Okay, now let's go to the beach," she said.

Much to Soledad's most playful dismay, as we walked along the main highway which was Highway 1, i suggested we should hitch a ride to a beach i was familiar with. The beach was secluded, and the sand was whiter than usual for a California beach. i didn't have to use much charm, for she folded under just one plea, and she agreed to hitchhike. If there is one place you can do this safely, it is amongst the free souls of Santa Cruz.

"It shouldn't be too hard," i said and placed my thumb out into the road as i turned my back against the wind. i felt Soledad press herself behind me along with the cool sea breeze that opened up my sinuses. Sure enough, almost instantly, an older Latino man wearing a plaid shirt and a sombrero pulled over in his old, beaten up pickup truck.

"Hola, Señor!" i said. He smiled and with his smile came hospitality.

"Where are you heading?" he said in halting English.

"Up the road a mile or so, heading to Davenport. Is that okay?"

"Sure, Amigo," he said, and as he smiled for a second time, i noticed his humble festering teeth. "Hop in the back."

i offered my hand to Soledad; she took it in aid for her to climb into the bed of the truck. i followed behind her. We sat against the cabin facing the open road that was being left behind. Left behind like broken memories with only pockets full of rain. i held Soledad as her hair waved freely in the wind. The perfumes of the breeze and her hair intoxicated me; i became mildly giddy as we approached Davenport.

i tapped on the cabin's rear window to signal our host that we could be dropped off. He pulled to the side of the road. i hopped off and assisted Soledad in her climb down. i walked over to the driver's window and offered my hand, and he gladly shook it and wished us farewell.

We crossed the two-lane highway into patches of trees and bushes that lead us uphill for a while. i worried for Soledad who was wearing something like Sunday School shoes, but she handled the little hike without a problem. Once we reached the top of the hill, we walked on an old railroad track that ran all along up and down the coast.

"Do you know where you are going?"

"i sure hope so."

She laughed. She always laughed, but that's not why i think i might have fallen in love with her. i hardly knew her; i just barely found out what her favorite color was. But through the power of prose and poetry that lay deep in her heart and mind, i was convinced that it was love that i was in. It had to be, what else could it be? Insanity?

But that's where it got complicated in my eyes. Although she was a great poet, she was also smart and beyond logical. i was so damn emotionally disturbed that my very life was my poetic delusion. Her life could probably be written in four hundred pages of vintage paper, and all i was able to write was an awful attempt at a single stanza. Although i had a prior publication, i was drowning in fear. And she was so full of hope and desire to write that i couldn't handle it at all. At least, i didn't think i could.

i grabbed her hand and led her into a field of grass and flowers that took us to the ledge of the cliff. The thunderous roar of the lonely sea grew louder and louder. We got to the ledge, and i let go of Soledad's hand for a moment and looked over the ledge. The massive waves foamed and broke on sharp black rocks to what seemed to be thousands of feet below me. i stepped closer to the edge, pieces of the ledge, rocks and dust broke off, and i watched them as they bounced off the cliff walls and pummeled all the way down and disappeared within the rocks and waves. With each crash of the waves there was a pounding drum beat that played along with my heart, beating from out of my chest like a bullet from a .38 special. i stepped even closer, and i felt the wind wrap around me as i leaned precariously over the ledge and began to fall. Soledad swiftly wrapped her arms around me and pulled me back from the cliff's edge.

My lungs were aching, but i pulled a cigarette from my pocket and lit it anyway. i avoided Soledad's eyes that were burning at the core of my chest and soul. She didn't say anything, but as she stood merely a foot from me, i felt the rhythm of her panting heart go with the pulsing of the rays from the sun. My smoke filled the air, and i couldn't smell the sea breeze; i imagined neither could she.

"Let's go." My words shattered the silence like a scream of a fallen angel.

We walked down the zig-zagging trail that lead us to the beach. As far as i knew, the beach was nameless, which was ominous but lovely like poetry itself. i walked ahead, and Soledad followed behind; every couple of steps, i would turn to her and try to smile in attempt to convince her that what she thought had happened on the cliff wasn't a reality, but she reciprocated with a saddened smile. In a weird way, she looked beautiful with that broken and sad smile; i suddenly had the inspiration to pick up the brush and have another go at painting, but that wasn't the time or place, so i tried to focus on the present.

The end of the trail took us between two giant walls that blocked any view of the beach and as we approached, i turned to Soledad and walked beside her. She didn't look at me, but i grabbed her hand anyway, and she didn't pull away.

We passed through the rocky walls and were greeted by the chilly sea breeze once again. She smiled and looked at me. i felt clemency flow from her smile. i saw the reflection of the sun in her eyes along with the horizon. i kissed her. We took off our shoes and socks and walked on the cool white sand. We strolled closer to the water where the mist wrapped us both in a cool blanketed comfort. The foamy, cold water chilled yet soothed our feet and toes as the sea rushed up the sand and dragged us back into her a bit. No one was around, just her and i. She stopped and faced the sea and the sun. i stepped back and saw her become a silhouette as the wind curled her hair around in the air, giving me a whiff of her that i loved. i didn't know what was going through her mind, and, in a way, i didn't care. It was probably none of my business anyway. i lit a cigarette. Her hair was a mass of dark shadow with golden highlights that danced along the painted wind.

"Look at this; can there be anything more marvelous than this?" she breathed.

Head down as i exhaled, the smoke curled around Soledad's curves, caressing her calves and slowly moving up towards her thick thighs and a lovely waist, something straight out of a painting. The gray and white smoke wrapped around her white dress that exposed her back just enough for my eye and finally the smoke tickled her neck with the gentlest touch like the caressing of a rose.

It is true what they say, "time flies when you're having fun." i never gave much thought to that saying; i often found it to be a cliché and a copout, but when the red, yellow and golden sky was seeing out the sun as it began its downward sail into the horizon and the hours whistled away in the chime of the wind, it's easy to feel the truth in it.

i smoked another cigarette and laid down on the sand. i was posed with my elbow dug into the sand as it held me up, one leg stretched out and the other in a triangle shape with my barefoot flat against the sand. Soledad was merely a silhouette as she tangoed along the shore with the water at her feet. Her white wide brim sun hat and vintage dress were still capturing the glisten from the sun. She glowed as if she were a ghost as her strong pose was threatened by the wind. She more than likely wanted me to dance with her, but i didn't want to dance, even if it was with her; i had tried dancing once and didn't like it. But she danced and would give glances towards me in invitation. She had discarded what had happened earlier on the cliff. She held one arm straight out and the other at shoulder height curled up with the mist from the surf as her partner. i smoked and enjoyed the sight of her carefree delight.

The day quickly became one of those grandiose days like those of the wind. One often forgets the simple things in life, and that is when we truly die. It is not in death when our souls leave this earth, in which we die. It is the very moment we begin to worry about worldly things and forget about the things like the wind, sunsets, and kisses.

i went into a daze as Soledad danced with the wind. i wasn't at the beach anymore; i had dropped a benny and was working vigorously at my typewriter. Turning out pages and pages between clouds of smoke and cups of coffee and whiskey. There at the beach i had an idea. Soledad kissed me and interrupted my thoughts. They disappeared in the cool breeze.

"What's wrong?" she asked when she noticed my furrowed brow.

"Nothing," i hedged.

She looked beautiful and i wanted to tell her that, but i didn't, even though i thought it would be acceptable. We were still relatively strangers. i didn't know her last name or her favorite dish. But perhaps because i knew her favorite color, it would be okay to use the word "beautiful."

We humans make our thoughts more complex than they need to be. We always doubt ourselves although we know exactly how we feel. It is absurd. And this absurdity is everywhere. Reality is just as absurd as an escape. The absurdity of reality lies within itself, we are never in control of anything even though we like to pretend we are.

And the escape, the escape is by far worse. When one escapes reality for a moment, one is but a fool. i am guilty of this, for i am possibly the greatest fool of all. An escape is a temporary solution for a temporary problem, that problem being life. One is often consumed with drugs and alcohol when we are better off being consumed by art and poetry, for they are the purest forms of escape.

i found myself thinking and asking myself if love was absurd? i wondered, "How could it not be?" but for the life of me, i could not find an answer to the question. But surely it must be. Any great romantic is a fool and any great fool is a romantic. This was a good explanation for me. i had lived my life in solitude, but i was a terrible romantic and the biggest fool i knew; i was the only fool i knew.

i flicked my cigarette away, grabbed Soledad and pulled her on top of me. i rolled over as her hat fell off; i held her in the sand and dirt. i could tell she liked me holding her but didn't like being on the sand, but i didn't care. i kissed her and wished that very moment that i would die, for it meant i would be in the presence of beauty and marvel at my final hour.

The sky grew darker, and the blueness of the sky was turning its usual purple with shattered rays of pink and gold. We climbed up the trail and were able to hitch another ride into downtown Santa Cruz where we had dinner at a local diner. i had steak and coffee, and she had a chicken dish and iced tea. i felt like we were locals although in reality we weren't really from that far away.

We walked from the diner to the train station, and we were able to catch the last train back home at ten o'clock. We sat on the upper level again, but there wasn't much of a view with the grand exception of the pale moon that left a trail of light that followed us all the way back home. The stars were really bright, brighter than any other night in these cities of ours. The train takes a little longer than a car ride so we arrived back in San Jose just before midnight. Soledad, again, slept almost all the way while in my arms as i replayed all that had happened that day.

The train came to a stop and i gently shook Soledad, she woke up. "Are we back home?" she asked.

"Yes," i said and then kissed her forehead.

We walked the streets in the midnight hour, again talking about nothing in particular. But the conversation would never cease. We would talk about anything, everything and nothing, and it would all make sense.

We never agreed to a spot where we'd be going, so, absentmindedly, i walked us to my studio apartment. The color of embarrassment blushed my cheeks.

"i wasn't thinking…i apologize."

She didn't say anything, as she looked my building up and down. Smiled. And then said, "Apologize for what?"

i opened the door to the building, and she walked in; i followed. We got into the elevator and reached my floor. i held the elevator door open for her as she exited. i walked her to my front door and unlocked it, opened it, and she stepped into the darkness of my studio. Because of her white dress and her hat in her hand, i could see where she was standing. i turned on the lights that dimly lit the room. Without saying a word she walked over to the window and looked out to the view. Although it wasn't much, she seemed to appreciate it. That's what i liked about her; she could find joy in the simplest of things.

She looked around my studio as i stood by my front door. She smiled at me. Then her eye caught my desk and typewriter. She walked over to it but didn't do anything. She just stood there and viewed all the books, but i knew she was interested in the typewriter.

"Go ahead."

She ran her hand and fingers over the keys. There wasn't a piece of paper loaded, but she hit the keys; i don't know what she typed, but she typed something out until she heard the bell ring. She laughed and then looked back at me. i smiled and then closed the front door. She continued to look around the studio and as her head slowly spun in curiosity, her body settled on my futon that was set out as a bed.

"Do you drink wine?" i offered.

"Sure."

"White or red?"

"Red is nice."

"Like the color of her lips," i thought but kept the words to myself. i went over to my kitchen counter that also held my wine rack. i grabbed a bottle, popped off the cork and poured two generous glasses. i walked over to Soledad who had made herself comfortable on my bed. i stood in front of her as i handed her a glass of wine. i sipped mine; it was actually a nice bottle i had been stashing for a while.

She took a sip and then gazed up at me. i sat down next to her and gulped my wine before i set the empty glass down on my nightstand. She handed me her glass where i placed it next to mine and when i turned back around to face her, she kissed me, a long, crazy and passionate kiss without an end.

i kissed her back as i placed one hand on her neck. Our mouths were like a rose with the petals intertwining. With my other hand, i ran my fingers through her hair as i laid her back on my bed. i was slightly on top of her; she felt my heat overcome her body and senses as our clothes rubbed against each other. We kissed. The French would be proud. i had one hand on her belly and i played with the ribbon that wrapped around her waist. i ran my hand up her body, feeling the texture of her dress over her breast.

She moaned, and this excited my senses, all of them. Her hair smelled like flowers after a rainy day in the spring; the image of her in my mind as we kissed brought tears to my eyes while my soft hands that brought much pleasure to my touch were caressing her warm body. But her moans! Her moans were like music; orchestras were playing, and symphonies were waiting to take the stage. Her lips tasted like rose petal infused red wine that was a joy to drink in abundance.

i kissed her long, silky neck. She tilted her head back onto my pillow as she felt my lips and breath on her neck. She maneuvered beneath me as i started to slip the dress straps down her smooth shoulders. i studied her face as she melted in my arms; her eyes were shut, and she was biting her bottom lip gently. i peeled off her dress, exposing her body, and i was drawn to her bellybutton. i kissed all around her navel as she raked her fingers through my hair. i could feel the heat radiating off her body and into mine. As my mouth trailed below her belly, she inhaled sharply and moaned with pleasure, hips rising to greet me.

# Part Two

i awoke to the rich aroma of freshly brewed coffee. The glare from the window was particularly heavy so i assumed it was almost noon, i wiped my eyes and placed my hand next to me where Soledad had slept. She was gone. i rolled over to my nightstand and grabbed a cigarette and struck it lit with a match. A deep inhale was all one could hear in the studio. The bathroom door was shut. i sat up on the bed and placed my feet on the cold floor and rubbed my eyes.

i didn't want to bother her while she was in the restroom, so i stood up and went over to the kitchen counter. There was a cup of black coffee that was half empty that was still steaming. i touched the French press with the back of my hand; it, too, was still hot. i grabbed a clean coffee cup, poured a little bit of milk in it and filled the rest of the cup with the coffee Soledad had prepared.

"Mmm..." i moaned as i sipped it. It must have been the best cup of coffee i had ever had. For the lone reason that Soledad had made it for me. i dragged my cigarette, held in the smoke and took a sip of coffee. "Yes," i thought to myself, "this has to be the best cup of coffee i have ever had."

i grabbed both cups of coffee and walked over to my bed. i placed the cups on my nightstand and brought the ashtray closer. Soledad couldn't be heard. i sipped my coffee and smoked, as my eyes lay dreamlike on the bathroom door. Nothing. i finished my cigarette and once again placed my hand over the bed where Soledad had nestled beside me; it wasn't hot but it was warm. But that could have also been my imagination. i got up and went to the bathroom door. i knocked three times, then knocked three more times on the door for Soledad and nothing. i gripped the doorknob and opened the door wide. She wasn't there.

"Naturally," i thought, "she probably went home." i didn't see a reason for her to be embarrassed of our intimacy the night before but i did find it odd that she didn't say goodbye. In a funny way the word "goodbye" had been my favorite word since the day i first got my heart broken by a girl.

i finished my coffee and had breakfast. i made myself an omelet with jalapeños, bell peppers and onions along with fried potatoes. i wasn't the greatest cook, but i never had to cook for anyone else, so my limited skills served just fine. i sat at my dining table and had another cigarette. i enjoyed the silence that the morning had to offer, but i wished i could have shared it with Soledad. i puffed out big clouds of smoke and through those clouds of gray smoke i noticed the dry flowers on my fireplace mantle.

i thought that very moment that i should surprise, or perhaps annoy, Soledad once more with flowers. i began to get ready. i hopped in and then out of the shower and was fresh as lettuce. As i got dressed, i received a call from Conor. "Damn." i didn't answer it, and he didn't leave a message. i went along my way promising myself that i would attempt to write something upon my return.

i exited out into the streets; good thing i was wearing an overcoat, it was sprinkling and i could tell there was more that the clouds had to offer. Quickly i walked over to a little market i knew that sold nice flowers. As i got there the rain had come down a little harder. It was such a difference from the day and night before. The lady that helped me pick a bouquet had been telling me how sad she was. Her husband had died recently, and she had to sell her little shop so she'd be able to bury him. i had no idea why she started telling me this; i was just looking at a bunch of marigolds.

"Those were his favorite...my poor Vicente," she said with a heavy heart.

What could i say to her? She was mourning, and the only thing i could offer was an embrace. Without me saying a word, she sobbed into my arms as i held a bundle of orange marigolds that were tied together with a silk ribbon. Oddly, i didn't feel that uncomfortable. This is where i felt the most comfortable, amongst those who suffer.

She cried in my arms for a while, i didn't care about the time. It is the least one can do when in those situations. Words although lovely to carve, can't always be curing. She was mollified a bit and backed away. With her head hanging low she pulled a white handkerchief from her pocket and patted her red eyes.

"Sorry young man...I'm terribly sorry."

"Not at all, Miss. i wish there was something i could do or something i could say to ease your pain, but i regret to say i can only offer my presence," i said as her attention turned to the flowers in my hand.

"Those are yours, young man, please take them."

"No Miss," i insisted; i pulled out some cash and placed it in her hand. She cupped my hand with both of her hands, grateful for the connection, no matter how fleeting.

"Thank you," she said as she fought back her weeping.

"On the contrary, Miss, i thank you, and i hope i have the fortune of seeing you once again." She accepted the payment as i placed a kiss upon the back of her hand and left the shop.

The rain had started to come down as heavy as the poor woman's heart who was in mourning. i wish i could have spent more time with her, but it also wouldn't be worthwhile for her; perhaps all she needed was someone to see her weep. It didn't seem like she had children, or friends for that matter, or they would have been there to support her. But this is how it is unfortunately. We get so wound up in our daily routines that we never stop to try to help an aching heart.

Ruminating on grief and loss, i arrived at the doors of the bookstore to find my Soledad. The overcast of the day muted the sunlight and grayed down all the colors in the town. i wasn't soaked, but i wasn't dry either. Marigolds in hand, i opened the door and walked in. The place smelled sullen, unlike before. i walked directly to the counter where another older lady who must have been in her 60's greeted me.

"Hello." i said oddly cheery, oddly for me. "i'm looking for Soledad. Is she here?"

She looked confused. "Who? Oh, she doesn't work here anymore."

i became even more confused. "What do you mean? Since when?"

"I'm not too sure about the details, but I'm afraid I wouldn't be able to tell you even if I knew. Are those for her?" she asked, nodding at the flowers in my grasp.

"Yes, yes they are."

"How lovely! Chivalry is alive and well, I am glad, but aren't those a little sad to be given to a young lady?"

"But what is love if not sad? A melancholy love is the strongest kind of love." She smiled in agreement.

"I'm sorry that she's not here; I wish she were. It's not every day a girl receives flowers nowadays. The youth don't understand courtship. They are too busy trying to explore each other's bodies without even knowing anything as simple as a favorite color. This is sad." She gazed at the forgotten souls there in the bookstore; once again, it was a lovely lady and i standing there.

"i wish i knew where she lived," i murmured, mostly to myself.

"A gentleman never asks that."

"Yes, i know; i was just thinking out loud. Can i ask you a favor, Miss? May i leave the flowers with you, and you can tell her they're from Juanito?"

She pondered on the favor i asked of her. She had a peculiar expression while she was thinking. She squinted her eyes that were being magnified by her thick glasses while she puckered her lips.

"I think you should hold onto them," she decided, "and when you see her, you can give them to her yourself. Since she no longer works here, there's no telling if I'll see her again."

i wasn't going to argue with her. She had a point. i turned around and looked down at my wet shoes, and within my shoes, i wiggled my toes around in my wet socks. i tried to think of why Soledad hadn't told me she had quit her job. i walked home in the rain.

When i arrived home i placed the orange marigolds on my fireplace mantle, then sat on my bed and lit a cigarette. It was colder than the day before, so the cigarette smoke warmed my lungs. i checked my phone but saw that i only had the missed call with no message from Conor.

i grabbed a bottle of Four Roses bourbon and a glass and sat at my typewriter for hours. Staring at the damned blank page. Hours passed, cigarettes were burned, and half a bottle of bourbon sunk into my belly. Night fell and the room began to spin, not a single word had been written, and only a murdered bottle remained, and i had blood on my hands. i struggled but was able to get up from my desk and made it to my bed. My head slammed against the mattress and i was out.

i woke up in the afternoon i believe. The sun was high in the sky and the shade well on her way. i lit a smoke, had a stiff drink while i brewed a coffee and checked my phone. Nothing except another missed call without a voicemail from Conor. i looked out my window; the day looked dark and desolate. No one was out and about; some shops looked closed. i poured some brandy into my coffee. The day was gloomy and passed rather slowly.

~~~~~

A few days had passed and not a word from Soledad. Part of me wasn't really worried, but the other part held onto hope while tangled in despair. There was nothing i could do without knowing where she lived or where she liked to go. All one can do is wait—wait for her return that may never come. My mind grew wearisome and dizzier with every bitter drink that i endured. Perhaps i was overthinking the situation; i always over-thought everything. The despair somewhat dispersed when i laid my head to rest. i rolled over to where Soledad had slept, and i could still smell the aroma of her hair infused in my pillow. i dug my nose into it and again took in a breath that soothed, not only my senses, but also, the loneliness in the room.

Saturday night i stayed up late into Sunday morning typing garbage on my typewriter. Sundays. i remembered the somber Sundays and how i had a disliking for them. But then i also remembered that i had seen Soledad at the Cathedral on Sunday. i downed a drink that made me weary and dreary, and i passed out at my desk.

i woke up right around the time that mass was beginning, so i decided not to waste any time. My heart had the deep desire to see her, to hold my Soledad, and i dared not lose a minute. i skipped on breakfast and my morning coffee. i just lit a cigarette and rushed out the door.

The town was lively, filled me with life. i wasn't running, but i wasn't letting anything slow me down. My cigarette cherry grew long as if i had been sharing the smoke. With my anxiety i lit another one as soon as i finished the first. Not soon enough, the Cathedral was around the corner.

The park across the street from the Cathedral had some kind of festivities going on with mariachi music playing and people dancing. This put a smile on my face, but i didn't pause to listen. i walked up the steps of the Cathedral, put out my cigarette, and opened the door.

Mass had started. Everyone was seated, and a chill that came from all directions embraced me. It was odd, and i felt it deep in my bones. i walked over to the baptismal, tapped the surface of the water with my index finger and blessed myself. i found a seat where i could sit on my own without disturbing anyone. i felt like a fraud. i should have been listening to the sermon, but i scoured the crowd of people for Soledad's face. It was impossible. Everyone was facing forward towards the preaching priest. i had no choice but to sit and listen.

A sermon about forty days and forty nights without water or food and only temptation as a companion was being told. Forty days and forty nights without food or water was nothing compared to forty days and forty nights in one's own mind with only the cold embrace of loneliness. i didn't want to believe that Jesus could survive such a thing. Not to be blasphemous, but because he, too, was also a man. Even as the Son of God, he must have felt emotional pain as well as physical pain. However, he'd also have that as an advantage; he wasn't an ordinary man like the rest of us. He had his father, God, on his side, and, despite my tendency towards despondency, i hate to believe that with as much suffering that goes on with humanity, we are forsaken.

Mass ended, and i was the first to exit the Cathedral. i went outside and waited at the foot of the step as i smoked a cigarette. Searching and searching, longing and longing, i sought her gaze and smile in a crowd of lonely people. i also searched for her mother, although i sensed she wasn't fond of me. i could at least know Soledad was here. Nothing.

A week, and what a long week, passed. Filled with memories and desire—the two elements that form time. Not a letter, not a call, no sight at all. It is a terrible thing to live with desire; a poor man knows it all too well. Whether it is a desire for wealth, health or love. One can only despair over one's own life, but it is best not to hope for a new life.

It is said that "time heals everything," but i must disagree. It will not heal cancer, and a depression from a broken heart might as well be cancer. It will slowly kill you without mercy, regardless of how much you had loved. If anything, the more you love, the faster it will kill you.

i received two back-to-back phone calls from Conor without messages, so i assumed whatever he had to say wasn't of much importance. i had nothing for him anyway, neither pages nor promises.

i thought about the older lady from the shop who was mourning her husband's death and how she was suffering and found herself alone until i had come along. She was so helpless, and this made me feel as if i, too, were mourning. Mourning the death of love, mourning the death of love that had grown so unexpectedly, so swiftly, deep in my core. With the love dying within me, my desire burned higher and hotter. Sitting up in bed, i gulped my wine, smoked my cigarette fiercely, and wept. i wept for the first time since i was a boy. It was almost unfair, not for me, but for my brother and mother. It had not been possible for me to cry over their deaths, yet here i was, weeping for a love that was only a few weeks old. The pain from a broken heart is immense and profound.

To make matters worse, when i woke up on the following Thursday, it was St. Valentine's Day. Painfully precious memories haunted my troubled mind. The indulgence of whiskey and wine barely took the edge off of my heart's lamentations hidden beneath my shirt. The wine brought the taste of her kisses upon my chapped lips. A blue Valentine's Day, that's what it was. The orange marigolds that lay in abandonment on my fireplace mantle had lost their color and had faded into a muddied brown hue. She had left behind the ribbon that lined her white sun hat where it lay on my nightstand. The whiskey stung the fresh cuts and open wounds that would eventually scar my heart. The ribbon was too much for me to look at, so i stored it in my nightstand drawer.

i found a couple of things in the drawer, nothing of value though: my blank address book and a bottle of lithium. The lithium tasted acrid, a dry and bitter taste, very metallic. i finally started feeling the warmth of the wine and whiskey in my empty belly, finally a warm comfort. i was dizzy. i drank even more. The cigarettes made me gag, but i fought through it. i tried to sit up on my bed but wobbled back and forth as i was tormented at the sight of the marigolds that were supposed to belong to Soledad. They reminded me of the death of the poor shopkeeper's husband, Vicente. The only thing i had inspiration to write was a eulogy, a requiem for the love that Soledad left shattered here on my hardwood floors. The room started to spin and blur. i knew with drunken certainty that the spirit of her memory would forever haunt me, and the loneliness born of her absence would be the specter in my soul evermore.

i believe Camus once said, "There is not love of life without despair about life." i agreed, but i also believed one cannot love without the despair of love. Love in its purest of forms is pristine, like that of a warm and caring love of a mother for her child. This form is almost always unconditional, but i regret to have used the words *almost* and *unconditional* in the same sentence when speaking of the love of a mother.

Then there is another pure form that is the love formed between two people that were at one time strangers or friends. This love is the most commercialized form of love; this, in its purest form, can become unrequited love, an absurd love. This is where one finds the meaning of an absurd love.

The absurd love is the most experienced yet goes unrecognized by mankind. This is why all romantics are fools. Love is absurd because it changes the way one thinks when one is madly in love. A person can act terribly unreasonable when he or she is in love, more often for a love that fails to reciprocate. The love naturally grows and grows with our imagination. We see the sunrise differently with radiant infatuation. One foolishly seals their heart with a kiss in vain and is left with a rose with a broken neck. i do not wish to speak ill of these romantic fools, for i am certainly a fool as well.

Smoke from a fresh cigarette sobered me up a bit, but i was all out of wine. i headed out of my apartment and onto the street. Stumbling and weary, i smoked and walked down the avenue to a little liquor store a handful of blocks down.

The day was gray and chilly; i didn't bring a jacket, and it started to sprinkle. The guy at the liquor store didn't want to sell me anything until i tipped him a couple of bucks. i got a bottle of wine and a *Benze* inhaler—a little "poor man's meth" for later.

i walked out the door with my purchases, and someone bumped into me. "Soledad," i thought soberly and quickly. i turned around quickly, a little too quickly for my inebriated state. It was the older lady from the shop, Vicente's wife. She recognized me right away, like one would John Dillinger in a mug shot.

"Sorry, Miss," i apologized somberly.

"Young man!" she said excitedly with her cracking and shaky voice. i hadn't noticed that she had lovely, sad eyes. For some reason her pale skin and rosy cheeks complimented her features. "Pleasure running into you."

"The pleasure is all mine, Miss."

i stumbled as she grabbed me by the forearms and shook me vigorously, like the way you don't want to shake a baby. She shook my arms; the bottle i was holding in my hand bumped her side. It was wrapped in a brown paper bag, but it was obviously a bottle of some sort of liquor. She looked at the bottle and then at me. i could tell that it saddened her. Her countenance grew heavy, and the wrinkles on her forehead that looked like smooth folded paper had gathered up. She softened her eyes.

"You're mourning," she said.

i didn't move, what could i do or say? i couldn't react; my emotions were drunk, not i.

"You poor thing." She embraced me, cradling my head against her small shoulder, and all i could do was allow her to do so.

"May I ask what you're mourning, boy?"

i realized i had the courage to admit that it was over a woman that i was mourning. It was because of a lady, because of Soledad, that i was mourning. i was mourning the fall of my pride, dignity and, of course, my broken heart. i had the courage to say that i was "dying for a woman's love," or "for a woman's love, i was killing myself." i felt i had lost the meaning of life when i could no longer have her kisses. But i didn't say that. i did something different; i lied.

"My mother" i said.

i wasn't exactly lying. i have never stopped mourning my mother's death or my brother's or my father's. Why should one try to stop mourning someone? When one ends mourning the dead, then the lost are both gone and forgotten. That's another reason i wanted to be a writer; before people forgot me, i wanted them to remember me for bearing witness to the absurdity of life and love, the absurdity of words about love.

"I'm sorry for your loss," she said. She seemed unsure, almost skeptical, about whether i was lying or not, but her tone was kind. She didn't let go of my arms as she pulled away. "Walk with me," she said. We began to walk down the street, heading the opposite direction of my way home. "What is your name?" she asked as we walked. i was to the outside of the sidewalk, and she just hooked her arm around my elbow. The streetlights started turning on one by one in a trail behind us.

"Johnny."

"Short for Jonathan?"

"No, long for Juan."

She chuckled and snorted. It was cute.

"You are mourning your mother? This means you loved her and this is good, but you do not weep as I mention her. This is either because you are embarrassed to weep in front of anyone, or you are done mourning."

i didn't say anything. i just listened.

"We all die; we all have to eventually do our duty and die, but when we die, that only means we physically die. We remain very much alive within the people who we love and love us. We keep living within the ones we truly touch." i patted her arm in agreement as she continued, "One is too often distracted by the absurdity of life that we forget all together the absurdity of death. Why one must die? Have you ever asked yourself that question? Being alive for one day is being alive for one hundred years when we are facing and approaching our final hour. Why must we get so used to all the beauty in life: flowers, music, art, the sea and the glorious days under the hot sun and have to leave it all for the unknown? We are meant to live and then die for that very moment where we wish we could have just another moment during a walk in the rain or in the sizzle of a kiss. To enter a heavenly slumber without our loved ones and the things we love, not materialistic objects, but those natural objects and places. The abyss is what is absurd; life is absurd, but the absurdity of death is much, much greater. Do you follow young man?"

"Yes," i said with a shaken and slightly disturbed voice.

"What is on your mind Juan?"

"Not really anything, Miss,"

i paused briefly, pulled out my bottle of wine, and attempted to open it up with my pocketknife corkscrew. She didn't say anything, but i could tell she didn't approve. i started taking sips from the bottle and then offered her some.

"No thank you. That'll kill you."

i looked at her in a way that one might have thought that she had offended me.

"That's not what I meant to say, young man. I guess I mean..." she paused and placed her thumb and index finger on her chin and rubbed it. "You mustn't rely too much on that stuff; it affects one's judgment."

i struggled but achieved to get a cigarette out of my pocket and lit it, all in one hand. "Miss," i said, but she politely interrupted me.

"Please, Juan, call me Remedios."

"Remedios," i repeated, quite a lovely name really. i smoked my cigarette and offered her one.

"No thank you, I quit." i placed the pack back into my pocket. "You know Juan, one must die to live, and some just exist while others live. You want to be the one who lives until the day he dies."

i slowed down my pace of walking and felt, now more than ever, the chill of that dark and cold Valentine's Day. i puffed on my cigarette and felt the heat wafting up from the cherry warm my cheeks. She reminded me a bit of my mother, although, there was no one like my mother. My mother understood my sense of humor without me even really telling a joke or laughing in her presence. Like my mother, Miss Remedios more than likely knew i was keeping something from her. We reached the end of the block.

"Here is where I leave you Juan."

i stood there and looked up at the street lamps and street names. The streetlight on the corner of 2$^{nd}$ and hope lit just as soon as we both stood beneath it.

"i insist, Ma'am. i'll walk you home; it is getting late."

"No, it's okay, young man; we both need some time alone."

i completely understood and agreed; that's all one can do when rejected in that manner. i took a sip of my wine as she turned and started to walk away. As she turned her back to me and took a couple of steps, my sips turned into gulps. i pivoted around and went home.

i arrived at my studio, smoking and with a half a bottle of wine. i brewed some coffee on my French press; the aroma filled the room, nudging out the stale scent of emptiness and old cigarettes. i poured myself a straight black cup of coffee and broke open the Benz inhaler. The stuff smelled vile, but i dropped the med-soaked cotton into my coffee and stirred it around. i took my coffee, wine and smokes to my bed and placed them on my nightstand. i knocked something over. i leaned over to pick it up, and at my feet was the full bottle of prescribed lithium. i picked it up and placed it on my nightstand next to my wine.

About an hour or so passed along with the rest of the bottle of wine and a dozen cigarettes. The Benze coffee was ready, and i drank the whole thing in one long draught. Not the greatest taste in the world, but i'm sure there are worse. The Benze battled with the tin of the lithium for worst aftertaste, but the coffee was a strong mediator.

i grew angry. Anger was an emotion i hadn't felt in quite a while. i often skipped anger and went straight to depression. i hadn't handled anger, and at that moment i didn't know how to. i had another cigarette, and then i started to feel the effects of the wine-Benze-coffee-lithium cocktail. Within about half an hour, i experienced a euphoric up and down effect. i didn't feel good—rather sick in the stomach, but i remained conscience. i went into the bathroom and stood in front of the faucet. There were two of me staring back at me from the mirror. i laid my head on the cool sink, only to raise it up and take three gulps of my mouthwash. It was like taking three gulps of fire, but it did its job and scorched out the bile on my tongue. i didn't know what i was angry at, but it wasn't Soledad. "i love her…i think," i thought to myself.

i walked back to the center of my apartment. As we all sometimes get during our drunken hours, i was stubborn and wanted to listen to music. i went to my record player and gave it a good dust off with my hands. i played with the lid, opening and closing it to hear the hinges creak. i picked up the needle and hovered it over the record that i had placed in there during my last forgotten drunken night. Billie Holiday. i spun the record with my hands without the needle touching the vinyl. i ran my fingertips over the musical ridges of the record. i closed my eyes. "Gloomy Sunday." The music, the horns, were being transmitted from my fingertips up my aching forearm, caressing my shoulder and finally gently whispering in my ear. Then the benny hit me hard.

i was having a rush and being dragged down at the same time. i switched on the record player and turned the volume all the way up. The music was playing faster in my mind, faster than it was. i stumbled to my bed and plopped down. Fucking nasty lithium crept up in the back of my throat.

i got really weary, really suddenly. The moon peaked into my room as my mind started to fog. An overdose of pleasure is always good; one sleeps profoundly until a heart is found. i will sleep to investigate the mysteries beyond. i'll sleep until i find Soledad's heart. i would wait all my life, even in her sadness, in her whispers and in her silence. i'll breathe in the desolation she left behind and exhale an essence. i shut my eyes. The music pumped in my head. Billie and her heartrending voice—she sang for me; i, too, would welcome angelic wrath to join my love. i knew this pain would evaporate when i stopped clinging to a waking life without her.

i soared over a foamy sea; i definitely dreamt, for man is not capable of these tremendous feats. i was weightless, light as a feather, as i floated within clouds that were softer than anything, softer than Soledad's skin in the sun. For the first time since my childhood, i felt innocent again. Dreams are so unpredictable; i went from soaring over the sea to running in hills of green grass and trees. My brother wasn't there, although, i felt his presence. i was carefree, much like a child, but i was a grown adult.

As i ran through the fields of grass, going up and down rolling hills, i looked up at a sky with a handful of clouds. i was fearless, and i realized that i should be. The sky is the one that should live in fear. It should tremble when two lovers vow to never part and when the universe is excited by a kiss.

The sun beat down on me, and i embraced it; i gathered as much sun as i could as i ran, passing by all the flowers that were like pretty girls everywhere. i wondered if we all had a sole purpose in life or a *soul purpose*. i came to the conclusion that my soul purpose, although i had evidence pointing to the contrary, my soul purpose was to love. And i wanted to love; i wanted to love my family, and i wanted to love Soledad. For my brother, mother and father, a love will always be present, but i wanted to love Soledad in the life i had, the life i lived. Before the sky would come down for us as it did for my brother, mother and father. i wanted to love Soledad before the sun died, and the moon lost its glow, and before the sea loses all form of compassion. Only in dreams would something like this be a certainty for any man. But in sunlit reality, it is possible but unlikely.

My dream quickly turned ominous. The sea turned violent and gray with thunderous crashes. The green grass had turned to a dry olive green and tan wasteland, and the trees turned their lively colors into dead falling leaves. i didn't know where to run or if there was any place to run to. The trees began to bend over and extended their naked branches in effort to grab me, and all i could do was run downhill. i ran into the sky that had become a dark gray; the clouds were streaked with white lightning and outlined in a smoky black mist. The birds had stopped their chirping and abandoned their homes and all hope. i began to run uphill; i ran as fast as i could. i ran with my eyes shut. The wind picked up and lifted me off my feet. The wind blew harder and faster until i fell. i opened my eyes, and i was falling down to the violent sea. A silent splash and i was in freezing water, pulled in all directions. My head popped out of the water. i was being dragged out to sea into the darkening horizon. Something grabbed hold of my leg and pulled me underwater. A mermaid, but with a gray-scaled tail and skin; i couldn't really see. i looked up at the disappearing light. It got dark, too dark, so dark i couldn't tell if my eyes were open or closed. i strained against the blackness filling my lungs, and then, nothing.

# Part Three

i awoke on an uncomfortable spring mattress that squeaked and groaned as i tossed and turned through the night. Everything was a blur; i couldn't remember a single thing. There was a small barred window almost at the ceiling that i couldn't reach even if i tried, and the place smelled stale. The lights were white and florescent, the walls also white; at least the floor was carpeted in a light beige, which was a nice break for my stinging retinas. When i finally came to, i realized i was at a hospital or rehab. This thought made my head ache.

A knock on the door sparked my alertness, and—for a split second—i thought it might be Soledad. Disappointment punched me in the gut. It was a nurse dressed in light green scrubs. i noticed her worn tennis shoes and her hair pulled back into a bun.

"Where am i, Miss?"

"You are in the hospital. You don't remember?" Her voice was clear and curiously flat but on guard, as if she were deliberately scrubbing it of any emotion until she knew how i would react to the information. i shook my head "no" and looked around once more—as if a second glance around could change my location or state of mind. The place was desolate and dark considering the amount of light that flooded the room. i ran my fingers through my hair as i tried to figure out how i ended up in this place. i thought intensely of Soledad; i wasn't able to even conceive that it was her ever-present absence that had brought me to the point of needing hospitalization.

Or maybe this was hell? "This must be hell," i thought to myself as the beams of sweat gathered along my brow. It was hot, hotter than i could imagine for a February day. That's if i had only been in this place for a matter of days. The sweat also gathered on the back of my neck and soaked into my shirt collar. No, not my shirt, hospital gown or scrubs. A quick check assured me i was still wearing my own pants. With the back of my hand, i brushed away the sweat from my forehead and nose.

"Do you need anything, Mr. Espiritu?" asked the nurse. i smirked at the manner she had addressed me; it was rather formal for the location we had found ourselves in.

"Cigarette? Can...or may i have a cigarette?" She enlightened me that hospital rules prohibit smoking on the hospital campus.

"But I can make an exception," she said with a conspiratorial smile.

"Oh? Why's that?"

She smiled and said, "I love your writing."

i was flattered but was unable to say a single thing. i hung my head down low and noticed my feet with only my socks separating the cool, soft carpet from my toes. It was nice to feel; i imagine anyone would be happy to feel just a single pleasurable thing in this place rather than discomfort.

i don't believe i was hungover, but i had a headache. i stood up and stretched my arms—up, out back—to see if i could still feel my blood moving; the nurse just stood there and watched me.

"Do you have my smokes?" i asked

"No," she replied, "but I have some."

She reached into her pocket and pulled out a pack of cigarettes. She popped two cigarettes out, placed one between her red lips and extended her hand out. i reached out with an open hand and the cigarette fell into my palm.

"A Lucky Strike. Why don't we get married right now?"

She smiled but didn't blush; she must have had heard that a million times before, especially at a place like this. "We need to smoke outside though," her voice was raspy. i liked it—a lot.

i grabbed the thin white blanket that i slept with and wrapped it around me.

"Good, you'll be fine. It's cooler outside. The air conditioning has been broken in this place for months." We made our way outside. We passed a lot of poor souls as we wended our way through the halls. i imagined everyone was ill but had no idea why we were locked away.

An old man i noticed reminded me of my father but was much, much older. His hair was all white and his old dark eyes that were like a dog's, sagged in reflection of the enthusiasm in the place. The air smelled even more stale and acrimonious than the room where i had awoken.

The old man's eyes were focused on a television set that was playing old novellas in Spanish. He looked so sad; i didn't know the meaning of that word, possibly, until my eyes witnessed this old man and the countenance that he wore. i kept walking until the nurse opened up the door that led to a small patio.

It was actually quite lovely and dreamy. The grass on a slight hill was as green as the grass in my dreams. There was a granite or marble bench for two that was at the corner of the three giant brick walls that were made to keep any brave person from attempting to escape.

i sat down at the bench; thankfully, it was cooler than inside the building. The nurse took out a matchbook from her pocket and as she about to strike a flame i grabbed the matchbook from her hand and struck the match. i reached out to light her cigarette first. She leaned in and allowed me to light it, and with the same flame, i lit mine. Without an invitation, or a gesture from me, she sat down beside me. i took a deep inhale and looked at her. She had burgundy-from-a-box hair and nice blue eyes that were deeper than the sky.

"Why am i here…?"

She looked at me, as she must have sensed i wanted to ask for her name. "Mary," she said, completing my question as she smoked her cigarette.

"You don't remember Johnny?"

i looked at the grass that gently swayed in the cool February breeze. It swayed, waltzing to the music played by the birds singing within the shadows of the trees sheltering the patio.

"No," i said. i just sat there, unconsciously swaying slightly with the tall grass as the sky grayed with gathering clouds. It almost didn't even really matter. i couldn't find my dear Soledad, and more likely than not, with my luck, she was in the arms of another man.

i wanted to write it all down in hopes that it would relieve some of the pain and emptiness. It was a pointless thought. Even if i had a blank piece of paper in front of me, i figured it was my turn to lose. i wouldn't even know where to start; i wouldn't have the words to fill the page. i just wanted the light of the moon to bathe me, drown me in its silver gleam. Silently, i lied to myself, "It was good, great even, while it lasted." i tried to convince myself into accepting…what? Her loss? My love for her? A life without her still worth living? Only time would tell what was true or false. Or, just maybe, time would give me the opportunity to write my truth, as absurd as it may seem.

i remember her barely tan, pale as the moon skin, and for a moment, i was able to touch her once more. Run my hands over her soft shoulders and down the curve of her hips as her hair flowed in the wind. She gave me a moment that i will never forget, but i hoped that even in her distance, she'd understand that, for the first time in a long while, i had succumb to my emotions. Here in this place, i was both in heaven and hell. Somewhere between the sea and the radiant sky. The seagulls would carry my heart to a new world.

"Johnny?" The pretty nurse interrupted my thoughts, which was probably a good thing.

"Yes?" i replied without glancing at her.

"You are here because you attempted to kill yourself. Do you have any recollection?"

i stayed quiet as i truly attempted to remember everything, anything, but the environment had thrown me off. "No," i said as she dragged her cigarette and French inhaled it.

"Your friend, Conor, brought you in. He told us he had found you on the floor of your studio."

My hands got clammy. i knew i didn't want to live, but i didn't really want to kill myself. i had always chosen the cup of coffee instead. But now, she claimed i had actually attempted to end my life. In an odd way, it didn't bother me. i hadn't cried at my brother's funeral or at my mother's, and yet i cried over the absence of Soledad? Nothing made much sense to me.

i guess it didn't really matter if i saw my Soledad again. i would still have the nostalgia of an intimate night with the shadows under a starlit night accompanied by a symphony of the midnight breeze. i was intoxicated by what was, apparently, unrequited love, but i knew that the last night i had spent with Soledad had changed our paths to our destinations. The romantic in me said, "i am no longer interested in love," but love itself will live within us in every poem and every star in the sky. i would have to die with only memories and nothing more.

"How long have i been here?"

"You came in last night, around three a.m."

i tried to enjoy what i could from the Lucky Strike she had given me, but it was sobering me up more than i liked. Even with the blanket wrapped tightly around me, i was cold. They had taken my shoes, belt, cigarettes and, worse of all, they didn't bother bringing me a bottle of anything. Even rubbing alcohol would do. We finished our cigarettes and ground them into nothing. The ashes and tobacco flew away with the wind.

"When can i leave?"

She slightly frowned as she replied, "You have to complete seventy-two hours of evaluation… so, at least two more days."

Two more minutes in this place felt unbearable-let alone two more days. She placed her hand on my shoulder, and i couldn't help but think that she wanted to have sex with me. i was sure that was my ego talking, but it didn't make a difference. Even if she did want to go to bed with me, i wouldn't really want to. It would never help someone that was suffering through loneliness; perhaps it helps for fifteen minutes, but, much like having a cigarette, it leaves you wanting more. One is never really satisfied with vices. i stood up and we both went back inside.

i was informed that breakfast was about to be served before the first therapy session of the day. As the nurses set up chairs in a circle in the middle of the living area, i helped myself to some coffee; it was surprisingly good. i didn't think a hospital would have a good brew, however, it was a classy brew. Unfortunately, due to the location of where it was served, it had to be the worst cup of coffee i ever had. Unsuccessfully, i tried to enjoy it. i was offered a menu to order some breakfast before the therapy session began, but i declined. i sat down in the circle of chairs, coffee in hand. The room was stifling. Outside was nice and cool, but inside was almost unbearable.

Some nurses rolled in flat carts filled with delicious smelling food. Some patients had ordered pancakes and eggs, while others ordered fresh baked pastries, hash browns, and omelets. i almost felt hungry but assuaged it with my coffee and the smell of cigarette smoke on my fingers.

Everyone ate in silence. i'm sure they were as uncomfortable as i was. i assumed that some of those poor people had been there several times before. They looked so accustomed to the routine and didn't seem bothered by being watched twenty-four seven. Although our treatment by the hospital staff was sympathetic, every sound and movement triggered my anxiety. i felt it unjust to feel as if my solitude was being perverted and forced into unwanted company. Not soon enough, breakfast was over, and a few counselors stepped in to join the nurses and patients. Therapy began.

~~~~~~

We were all reminded of our hopelessness and alienation, which seemed counterintuitive; it appeared we had to head further south before we could head north. Everyone started to perspire even more. As i looked around the circle, I witnessed my familiar tics mirrored in others: heels bouncing, fingers drumming, glances averting. The counselor was speaking into increasingly heavy air. The beads of sweat on my forehead and brow slipped one by one into my eyes. i squinted with the sting of the liquid salt that further irritated my red eyes. i blinked the sting away and rubbed my eyes as the room became blurry. i couldn't say what the therapy session was specifically addressing, but some patients were in tears.

It appeared that i tried to end my life; i couldn't agree nor disagree with that notion. i felt that i didn't really belong there. i was depressed, possibly suicidal, but a terrible pinch of hope was still deep inside me. Not to say that the other men and women weren't hopeful. i just felt i had a better grasp on hope than they did. But, i've been a fool before, like all romantics before me. All romantics were fools. Fools to believe in love, fools to have hope for love, and fools to be love itself.

Therapy ended; we weren't allowed to know what time it was. i asked the nurse for another cigarette; she obliged me. i grabbed another cup of coffee and went outside onto the patio again. Mary walked outside with me. We sat at the bench once more, and we smoked our cigarettes in silence for a few moments.

"You are awfully quiet, Johnny. I never thought I'd meet you, but I figured you would be a bit more loquacious...you know, talkative."

"Yes, i know the word. i'm sorry to disappoint," i said as i observed the smoke slowly escape through my mouth and nostrils. She laughed at my sarcasm; that was my type of girl. i looked at her for only a second, i couldn't stand to have to endure any more beauty expelled through the eyes and smile of a feminine spirit. It just wasn't fair. It's my idiotic opinion that women have it easy. All they have to do is smile, and they can have the world on a bended knee; they can be any man's wife.

"Why did you have to come here?" she asked; i almost believed she was truly worried.

"It's complicated," i puffed through the cigarette.

"Was it because of a girl?"

"Deeper than that."

She didn't seem to know what i meant; she held the cigarette to her lips as she pondered. i knew she wouldn't understand, it's not because she was a woman but because of my inability to express what i felt. Ironically, i started to feel detached from my emotions. This turned out to be, i learned just moments later, to be completely false. i was completely aware of my emotions and was at the mercy of them.

"But it was because of a girl...a woman?" She shattered the silence as i thought long and hard on her question. i was never any good being interviewed.

"No, it was because of me...only me."

i didn't really know why or how i was pushed so far as to end up in suicide watch. One should, or does find comfort in the unknown. Knowledge is beautiful, but is also equally dangerous. One shouldn't be at the mercy of unbridled emotions. We should not only be in control of our emotions but also have the capability to manipulate and play them. There is an upside; fortunately, for me and the other patients, we are in touch with our emotions, therefore we can succumb to hope.

We finished our cigarettes, and i reached out to shake her hand; she bypassed my offer and embraced me. i let her hug me. She passively rested her cheek against my chest. i placed my chin on the top of her head and closed my eyes. Naturally, i took a breath and took in a piece of air that carried her perfume. For the moment that the darkness blanketed my eyes and conscience, i pretended that i was in the arms of Soledad.

"Don't worry, Johnny; pain is a passing thing. Yes, a lot of people who come here come back in the near future, but that is not a bad thing. Get help when you need help; put it in God's hands."

i bit my tongue at the notion of putting it all in the hands of God. That was the last thing i wanted to hear. It did, however, remind me of my mother, and i pretended she was there with me. That thought helped to ease my anxiety slightly. i excused myself and went into my assigned room. i tried to get comfortable, as comfortable as one can get while potentially being watched through a door with a window. i laid down and faced the wall. i shut my eyes only for them to shoot open with the sound of knocking on the door window. Those three shallow yet thunderous knocks pounded along with my heartbeat.

"Johnny?" Beyond Mary's voice, i felt the presence of another person. "There is someone here to see you."

i rolled over to find a priest standing in the doorway. i sat up on the bed, and the nurse left the room. i felt the density and sound of DOOM as she shut the door behind her.

"Hello, Johnny, my name is Father…"

i was listening with a filter of "who gives a fuck?" and bypassed little details like his name. He began to pace the room passively, not too much, just the normal amount to frustrate me.

"Father…"

He stopped his pacing and looked at me with a stern yet innocent face. He looked worried, and since we didn't know each other, i knew he wasn't necessarily worried for me.

"Why do i deserve the generosity of your visit?"

"Your friend, Conor, asked me to pay you a visit. He thought you'd like to speak to someone. He is worried about you." i merely blinked at him. "He said you were Catholic."

"i was raised Catholic, " i clarified, "that isn't entirely the same thing."

"No, I suppose it's not." He looked offended, but he didn't exploit it. i also didn't really want to offend him, or anyone really; i just didn't want my state of confusion to worsen because of what he might have to say. He crossed his arms as he asked, "Can I get you anything?"

"No. No, thank you."

"Coffee maybe?"

"Would you happen to have a cigarette?"

"How about we talk first, and then we can step out for a cigarette?"

i nodded my head in agreement. He was probably just being cordial; that's what the kindhearted do. He pulled up a chair to face the bed and sat down, not too close.

"Why did you decide to try to end your life?"

"i don't know...i didn't exactly...i don't know, i don't know anything."

He studied me very carefully. i didn't feel like talking to anyone. i felt desperate. i would have gone as far as marrying Soledad, tried to buy a house i couldn't afford, or would have successfully killed myself. It all weighed equally in my mind. Whether i tried to kill myself or not, i didn't succeed, and it proved to be embarrassing. i felt as if i were a failure, for i failed to kill myself. i was embarrassed to have failed or to even have attempted suicide. i still wasn't certain whether i had actually tried to kill myself or just kill my pain. Either way, i convinced myself that there was no shame in attempting. Whether or not this is true, i don't know, but it was the best conclusion i could think of, and that bought me the smallest drop of peace.

"Father, with all respect, i do not feel comfortable enough to speak to you, much less on this personal a matter."

"My son, I can assure you that you can put your trust in me, and you can be forgiven."

"Forgiven for what?"

"Attempting suicide, of course. The Lord knows your pain, but He can only relieve it if you ask Him for his exculpation with concession."

99

i stared at him blankly. Automatically, i assumed he wouldn't understand. He wouldn't understand the pain of being a man in love or the pain of love lost. Nor would he understand my view on priests.

~~~~~

When i was a boy, i regularly went to church to confess my sins. As children, my brother and i were taught to always trust in God and the men in the clergy. i understood this to mean to respect pastors and priests, but not glorify them as if they were holy. i was naïve. i looked at men of the cloth to be saints until one summer day in my thirteenth year.

My mother had taken my brother, cousin and i to church one Friday afternoon. It was hot and uncomfortable, a sardonic sign. My cousin had entered the confessional first; she apparently hadn't sinned much, for she exited quickly. She was given a day's worth of Hail Mary's for her troubles. My brother went next. i didn't have a clue of what he could have confessed to; he always treated me kindly and was obedient to our father and mother. He exited the confessional with a smile and held the door open for me. i entered the dark room with wooden walls and a little red light above the door. i sat on the uncomfortable seat and looked up at nothing, silently blessed myself, and looked at the silhouette of a man in black through the privacy of the fuzzy fence that divided us.

"Bless me father for i have sinned…"

He interrupted me, "What are your sins?"

i didn't expect a rude welcoming. i expected him to greet me and make me feel like i was at a holy place where souls could be forgiven. i was unsure how to answer, so i sought quietly for a response. Because of my silence, he grew agitated.

"Have you lied?" he asked.

"No, Father," i said with a cracking voice.

"You are a liar," he accused. i didn't say anything back. "How could you not have lied? Every boy lies."

"But i haven't father. At least, i don't remember," i conceded.

"You don't remember your sins, and you have come to confess them?"

"No, that isn't what i meant." i was becoming flustered and frustrated. i couldn't find the words to explain what i meant, but it seemed the priest wanted to keep me off balance.

The tension thickened the air of the little confessional booth. Every single breath was heavy as smoke. i started to choke on my apprehension.

"If you lie to me, you will be punished in eternal flames."

i was flattened by fear. i didn't understand why he was attacking me; what was so evil about my existence that deserved eternal retribution? i received no answer that day nor any day since.

~~~~~~

Under the harsh fluorescence, the priest sat patiently across from me as he waited for a response.

"i just wanted the pain to stop...all of it."

i didn't expect it, but he looked at me with contentment, and that made me smile. It brightened the moment and the trajectory of the day. How strange that the approval of this stranger had this effect on me. After all these years, i was still trapped in that confessional box, but this friendly priest opened the door to let in fresh air. Only twenty years too late, but what the hell, right?

Just then, a knock on the door announced the presence of another visitor. The priest stood and opened the door, blocking my view along with my curiosity. It was

Conor. It felt as if i hadn't seen him in years. He was a thin, tall man with blue eyes and dirty blonde hair. Although, i liked him and viewed him as a friend, i always teased him that his glasses made him look like a dork, and that i couldn't have a dork representing me.

The priest stepped back towards the bed and reached into his pocket. He pulled out a small card of some sort and a pack of cigarettes. He handed me the card. It was a St. Michael prayer card. i studied the card, saluted him with it, and placed it in my pocket. He opened up his pack of cigarettes and handed me one. i gladly accepted it. He patted me on the shoulder and glanced at Conor as he went on his way.

"Conor..." i stood up, and we greeted one another with a hug.

"Sorry I couldn't come sooner, I had some business to take care of."

i tried not to think much of his comment, but naturally, i couldn't help it. i placed the cigarette between my lips and silently mentioned to myself that i, too, had some business to take care of.

"Shall we step outside?" he asked. We walked out of the room where i was being kept, and i watched him observe the environment and the other inmates...patients. He seemed saddened by the place but kept any words and feelings to himself. We exited to the patio—a relief from the stuffy indoors. i sat on the cold bench; Conor stayed standing. He pulled out a matchbox from his pocket and tossed them at me. They landed on my lap. i tore the filter from the cigarette and placed it in my pocket; i would've felt terrible if i were to flick it into the granite bird bath that was a few feet from the bench. i lit my cigarette. Conor sat down next to me, however we both avoided eye contact.

"I need to talk to you Johnny, but first, how are they treating you in here?"

"They're nice."

"That's good…" He took a deep breath, "There's no easy way of saying this Johnny. I love you; I'm your biggest fan…"

i tried to interrupt him and spare him his troubles, but he continued to speak.

"I need to let go of you as a client." Smoke wafted between us. "My boss has been on me, and I know this is a hard time for you…"

i stood up, placed my hand on his shoulder and looked him straight in the eyes, "It's okay." His face didn't show much emotion, but i didn't need it to. i haven't been writing, and our relationship was just business.

i didn't want him to say anything else. There was no use explaining how a friendship had never developed. Any other words he would speak would be a waste of his breath. i didn't hate him, but i also didn't expect him to ever contact me again. i pondered on how he never invited me over to his home for a cup of coffee or to meet his wife. Most people assume friends have a price, but they never settle the value of one.

He stood up and straightened out his sport coat. i kept looking at the cracks on the ground with little blades of grass growing from them. He patted my shoulder, and i heard his steps dissipate as he walked away. i didn't look up, but i knew he looked back at me from the door that lead to the hospital corridors. i smoked my cigarette.

~~~~~~

A few hours passed, and the dark sky brought a small amount of relief from the heat indoors. Menus were once again handed out to all the patients; i decided it best to eat. i ordered a tri-tip sandwich on sourdough along with a salad, ginger ale and decaf coffee. Half an hour later the meals were rolled in on flat carts. No one really spoke; we all gathered around for our meals.

My plate looked great. Although i had a bad sense of smell, i dug my face into my plate and took in a big whiff of my meal. The bread smelled freshly baked and, i could smell how moist and salty the tri-tip was. Alongside my sandwich was my salad and salty potato wedges. i leaned back, picked up a crispy looking french-fry, dipped it into ranch and ate it. The oil sizzled on my tongue. i looked around and watched the others eating their hot meals; i was saddened.

Everyone had their heads down as they ate in silence. i didn't possess any form of animosity or revulsion for their demeanor. i was drowning in my own sorrow and guilt. My guilt manifested from the core or my existence and the fact that i had a reason to be there, and my reason wasn't at all different from theirs. My sorrow came from the overall fact that i wasn't the only one that decided that life wasn't entirely a rose but more like a weed. So many broken spirits in one room, eating dinner, as if playing the role of "being alive" would make it true. Perhaps it would. As deep in the gutter that one can be, one can always look at the black sky and warm themselves with a blanket of stars. But the core of my sorrow could be summed up in one word—innocence. As they ate, i looked upon their woeful faces, and their innocence brought tears to my eyes. i realized that if one ever has ill feelings towards another, one should see the other person's innocence and let themselves burst into tears.

After dinner, free time was the apparent routine. They put on a family rated comedy, but no one really paid much attention, so the nurses played old records. They played some Italian *tarantellas*, and it was amusing to see an old man, who struggled to stand up, tango the night away without a care. i enjoyed myself; i didn't have a choice.

i glanced around the room at the assemblage of lifeless souls, with the exception of the old man with a tango in his heart. "i'd like to know their secrets, all of their secrets," i thought. The group of nurses turned into a sewing circle while the patients were merely present. At least we all had full stomachs.

All these people might have actually known why they were stuck in here. i wondered if they knew and if they cared. i started to feel like maybe it was i who knew yet didn't care. My thoughts became heavy after dinner, and i grew tired, so i left the partying to the others and headed to bed. It was a nice and cool February night. i didn't dream.

When the day broke, i awoke on my own and just lay in bed. The walls were bleached-bone white; I felt a new, unwelcome, discernment of the term "rib cage." You think they would paint the walls, add a plant and a maybe Monet print, but nothing of that sort was attempted. The room yearned for vibrant life—like all of us. Maybe the room itself was also a casualty of the absurdity and pain of this life.

The nurse finally came in to wake me and was surprised to find me already awake. i wished she would have been prettier.

"Good morning, Juan. It's about to be breakfast, and then you have an appointment with the psychiatrist."

"Okay," i said as i sat up. i needed a shower but was deprived of that as well. By my second day there, i noticed that the stuffiness of the place along with everyone's natural fragrance all combined, made the place smell something sour and awful.

i got some coffee and put in my order for breakfast. i sat on the couch and looked out the window; it was raining. From indoors, i could imagine the smell of the wet flowers that were along the bed of the patio walls. The petrichor, such a rich, dark scent that fills the air, testified that California's clouds could still weep. One cannot replicate the perfume of heaven.

The room was surprisingly louder than usual; the nurses and patients had started to speak to each other. This hadn't occurred before. i was annoyed. Being kept in an uncomfortable place would annoy anyone. All the voices and chatter were a discordant symphony. Several voices would start to crescendo, while others faded. The drumming of syllables clattered sporadically in a strident imitation of the drop-drop-drop of the rain on the windows.

Eyes closed, i envisioned the drops of rain gathering in the storm drain. The teardrops of rain fell into a puddle by the green grass. The tears of rain thundered through the corridors and penetrated my chest. Opening my eyes, i walked to the door; it started to rain harder. i could see the little puddle by the green grass where the rain was gathering. The metronome of a heart that was hidden in my chest was in perfect time with the raindrops.

A nurse tapped my shoulder. My breakfast was ready. i sat down and sipped my coffee as i received my plate. Medium rare steak and eggs. The steak looked bloody, grilled and juicy. i reveled in the aromas of salt, pepper and the lime of the steak. i played with the yolk of the two sunny-side-up eggs with my plastic fork. i learned quickly why one laughs at a man who orders a steak at the fifty-one-fifty psych ward; they don't even hand out plastic knives.

After breakfast, i was taken to meet the shrink. An analysis that was far overdue and premature at the same time. Overdue, for my knees had buckled from a blow delivered by self-pity, and yet premature, for i regained my equilibrium. The walls were a dark maroon, and there was a large window behind the desk that offered a view of a giant white wall. The inside walls were decorated with paper awards. There was a wall of books; none were fiction. One cannot study one mind and expect to have the capability to understand many minds. The intellectual mind, marvelous no doubt, can be logically predictable. The creative mind, on the other hand, is an evolving mind; a kaleidoscope is not a good subject for strictly logical study. The enemy of the intellectual mind is, in fact, another intellectual mind. However, the creative mind is both logical and artistic; its greatest enemy doesn't lie amongst other creative minds but within itself.

The doctor came in. Dr. Montague. He was about six feet, 160 pounds, clean shaven with dark hair and thick dark eyebrows that were slightly obscured by his silver rimmed glasses. He was young to be a doctor.

"Let's see," he said as he walked in with his face in a folder that bore my name. He didn't greet or acknowledge my presence. He sat down at his desk and flipped through the tan paper folder with about half a dozen sheets of paper inside. "You are here because you attempted suicide by drinking in excess, taking prescribed drugs in excess along with indulging in some form of stimulant in excess. Does that sound correct?" He finally looked up at me. i already didn't like him.

"i don't remember."

"Well that's why you are here; you have to remember."

"i don't. i don't know what to tell you doctor."

He became agitated but kept his cool. He stared at me, and i became convinced that he didn't like me either. i had that effect on some people, maybe? i could piss people off. He reclined in his seat.

"Let's start on a different note; what do you do for a living?"

"What do i do for money you mean?"

"Yes."

"i'm a writer...or i used to be...it's complicated."

i was unsure but i felt like he wanted to hit me. He seemed like a smart guy but he was wound up tightly. He tried to get me to talk about what had happened, but i was able to do what people do, and that was lie.

It's not that difficult to talk about suicide. It just depends with whom the conversation is taking place. The best person to have a conversation about suicide with is yourself. Everyone else will only have the same opinion, the common opinion. This isn't entirely a bad thing, but when all read from the same greeting card, the conversation grows stale. Suicide is a topic that can get you through a dark night. Choosing whether or not to kill yourself is the most important decision one will make. The subject would be the most interesting if emotion could be taken out and replaced with logical thinking. This is where the absurdity of life makes itself known. The very fact that one is in a position where they question whether to kill themselves or have another cup of coffee is absurd. This does not mean one condones the act of suicide, for the act is a single person's decision and is often a silent one. i will always be on the side of life. And if i were to die by my own hand, i would have lived my life until that very day.

These conversations could not be between a patient and a psychiatrist. A suicidal conversation requires a creative mind with an intellectual thought. Whether or not i tried to kill myself is something the doctor will never understand. Not until he experiences the feeling, when one is pushed to the edge; not by society, not by somebody outside of yourself, but by your own mind. The fifty minutes in which the doctor was to get an understanding of my mental state proved to be futile. i didn't really speak and didn't pay any attention to anything else he had to ask. As i sat there, a pensive mood allowed me to paint a landscape on the wall outside the window. Unlike a man, a landscape lends itself to perception. After that meeting, i wanted to go home.

i was escorted back to the watch area, and i had another cup of coffee as i sat in a seat by the window and just watched the blossomed tulips catch and consume the rain. The rest of the day went by slowly but the sight of the rain was enough for me.

~~~~~

i was in bed with my eyes wide open to get a glimpse of the moon passing by my lone window. The chirps of what I made out to be at least three crickets that stood at the windowsill broke the silence. The chirps were loud and i was sure they could be heard through the corridors. i never knew why crickets would chirp and play their somber music in the still of the night until it dawned on me. They were lonely creatures. Their very nature was to seek and find companionship. They live an absurd life not so different from our own. This fact is unsurprising due to the incomplete metamorphosis that some men undergo in moments of despair. The crickets, as well as the cockroach, know the process all too well. To transform into an incomplete creature is as natural as it is tragic.

The chirps were melodic and somber, similar to the likes of French singer Edith Piaf. For a moment i found myself in a trance where their musical chirps vibrated from my troubled mind throughout my weary body. Three crickets chirping suddenly turned into two crickets and yet the music stayed strong. i was in bed looking at the ceiling and resting my hands on my belly, i lifted my index finger in the air and waved it around. Conducting the tiny violins chirping. The second cricket hopped off the windowsill and the last cricket played on without discouragement. "Any minute now," i thought, "He will find his companion."

The cricket stood lonely on the windowsill. i worried that it was chilly out that night. Interesting position to be in—worry for the condition of an insect, but, as his chirps bounced off the walls of my lifeless room, my heart suffered from palpitations of discomfort at the realization that this cricket was enduring a dark and chilly night. Forsaken under the moonlight and the stars that held his doom. He played on, as if hopeful that there was a crickette somewhere to sooth his soreness from chirping all night. i, for one, did not hold such hope.

i didn't find it helpful or necessary to hold onto hope for the idea of love or companionship. Solitude and loneliness can be vicious lovers, but they are lovers that can always be found. When one's friends abandon one, it is in solitude where one can find a remedy to the sufferings. Many people fear solitude, and most succumb to their tearful emotions when they realize that they are lonely. i suffered from bouts of depression and often medicated with fine wine and whiskey. However, in these depressions, i never once felt lonely; i felt awful and suicidal; the darkness that possessed me often overcame my senses, and i became blinded from the beauty that can be offered by, not only life, but by mother earth. Humans should compare their lives to the life of a cricket or a cockroach; only then will they completely understand their human condition and become comfortable with their core misery.

As i lay in bed wide awake, i listened to the cricket as the moon slowly made its way across the night sky. i ruminated over whether my life was any different than that of the lonely cricket. i had come from an egg and spent most of my immature insect years trying to make sense of existence and asking why suffering had to be a big part of our condition. There are many types of suffering that mankind and insects endure: abandonment, illness (both physical and mental), love, loss and death. It wasn't until i compared my life to the cricket's life, that i became aware of how much the cricket would find death to be absurd as opposed to life. If one creates music when times are at their worst, then they must live in hope, much like the cricket.

Hours went by and the cricket never once stopped chirping. "I should not stop chirping," I thought to myself. Suddenly my heart had opened up to the dispassion of, not only the world, but of our decisions to not truly live our lives. I knew at that moment that I was that lonely cricket that stood at the windowsill and chirped late into the night. I chirped for the sake of everyone else. And only when the sun has risen, will I have completed my duty.

I sat on the windowsill and faced the sparing purple and orange colors that smeared across the horizon and chirped away without a care in the world. To be happy, one cannot seek it. One merely becomes comfortable enough to become happiness. What seemed to be a million crickets joined in with me as I chirped to the sunrise. Playing and chirping with my cricket friends as the moon hid behind the mountains,          a          new          day          began.

# Part Four

The following days went by rather quickly, and my release day finally presented itself. I stepped out into the living corridors and just soaked in the life that the other patients had to offer. The energy was surprisingly tremendous. My head filled with light as my body absorbed the vibrations. I served myself some coffee and started to fill out my card for my breakfast order. The nurses stood together, away from the patients, as I tried to enjoy the coffee the best that I could. Breakfast was brought in, in its regular fashion. I received my plate of French toast and two sunny-side-up eggs. I ate and drank more coffee.

I was released. The farewells that I bid to the hospital staff were vague but heavy with gratitude. When I exited the hospital doors into the street, a different sun greeted me. It anointed my shoulders and head with warmth. For the first time in what seemed to be in a very long time, I heard and enjoyed the songs that the birds sang amongst the trees, although, I still saw a plethora of shadows amongst the brightness of the day. I stood on the sidewalk and soaked in the freedom—not only the freedom from being released, but also a freedom of myself, from myself, and let the breeze run the back of its hand on my cheek.

I stopped at a liquor store on the walk home and picked up some smokes and wine. The clerk was going about his routine, oblivious to the palpable *sonder* I felt for him and others. I, for one, was aware and sparred heavy rounds with my humanity; with every stranger that passed me, my chest and head were heavy with the burden of curiosity, thirsty for their stories, their hopes, dreams and despairs. The smoke filled my lungs, and I exhaled a cloud of new beginnings with the tar of memories.

The walk home was sobering. I built up a little sweat that collected itself on my brow and lower back. I viewed the neighborhood and the family owned shops with new eyes, and in turn, this gave me a new appreciation for them. I put out my cigarette when I reached my building. I looked up at its edifice and was blinded by the sun. I looked down at my black, worn out shoes and consciously entered the building.

I opened my front door, and although it was bright outside, my room was dark. The sunlight struggled through the drapes. I stepped in. I glanced around the room as I sat on my futon. An echo of sadness began to grown inside me. "Will I ever escape her...or them?" I thought to myself. I admitted that I missed her; I missed her essence even more so. Even in my thoughts, the trace of her smile and laughter that were once possessed by my life and studio still lit up my room. I placed the bottle of wine and my pack of smokes on my nightstand, kicked off my shoes, and let myself fall on my bed. I slept.

I awoke to my room reddened by the descending sun, and when I listened closely, I could almost hear the cricket that sang from my windowsill at the hospital. I felt his essence become my essence. In the darkness of my room that possessed me just as much as solitude, I felt the cricket that lived inside me play his chirps. And like that last night in my hospital room, the cricket played on. He kept playing his somber melody throughout the night. He kept playing as others ceased their music, as if he played in despair as his hopes burned to steam in the moonlight.

~~~~~

I felt well when I left the hospital but once again started to struggle with reality. I was alone. I felt it even more so than before. Nothing was left, no God, no purpose. All that remained were illusions. Like the cricket, regardless of the presence of hope or not, I will sit on the windowsill of the world, and I will chirp for all creation to

116

hear. I won't chirp in hopes of finding a companion; I will chirp for those that are in need of company in the middle of the night.

Darkness battled the hope that was germinating within me. The invincible summer that I had found within me earlier that day began to be tested and looked vulnerable as it entered the championship rounds. I knew that was the moment I would decide whether to be the controller of my own destiny or if I would once again succumb to hope and live through another winter with a burning but dying summer's sun in my belly. I popped open the wine and lit a cigarette. It is true; it does take more courage to live than to kill yourself. I made a decision, and on the morrow, the witness would be the sea.

I gazed at my abandoned passions scattered around the room: lifeless paints, empty brushes, mute musical instruments, and an orphaned typewriter that seemed to have not been used in a lifetime. I realized that I had long been a slave to my emotions—all expressed in different creative mediums over the years. It's a terrible thing to be a slave to one's own emotions. Suffering can either build grace and courage or drive someone mad. The poor Vicente's, the shopkeeper and the painter, both found their way beyond this suffering.

To be free of one's emotions would be ideal. However, one who believes it possible to be completely freed from their volatile and paralyzing emotions is mistaken. Every human is a free agent in this world, where he or she can make their own decisions and be happy on their own terms. One has to imagine oneself happy. There is trickery in the way artificial contentment is sold to us in the form of our "wants." One cannot buy serenity; one has to simply be content.

I was terribly troubled by the fact that hope has to exist. If mankind did not feel suffering, there would be no need for hope. Hope can be a beauty in the eyes of the beholder, but one must also question the existence of hope if one is to philosophize on the existence of mankind. I looked out my window down onto the streets. My chest burned with a melancholic oil when I mentally transcribed the story of every passerby. Transfixed by the smallest details, I found myself lost in *ambedo*, each leaf fluttering in the breeze—a galaxy, each person—a universe. As a reader and as a writer, I always found comfort in the works of fiction—the lies in which the truth is told. But fiction comes from the imagination, from the same grain as does comfort. The escape I experienced with wine and whiskey was fiction, but the quintessence of my escape was my greatest work of fiction.

It's difficult to live in hope, but I don't know another way to live. When someone declares suicide to be their destiny, I assume that, like me, they hope to find the peace that couldn't be offered in life. When I have contemplated suicide, I always hoped that I would find peace. Peace in a place where stars exist. I hoped that I wouldn't end up in a place with no music, no art, absent the sea and warm summer nights. I dwelled in this type of hope, not faith, a scary hope, yearning for armistice in the unknown. All the hope in the world can't keep everyone alive, but when there is great suffering, there is also great hope.

I did have hope, and it was slowly killing me. I had hope that I would be content with or without Soledad. I hoped for this hope to cease sooner rather than later. The solitude I once possessed was altered when my solitude was in the conscience company of Soledad. I didn't hold antipathy towards Soledad. My deep, obsessive love of her essence was enough to keep love alive. I knew that I would never see nor hear from Soledad again, but the intensity of my ardor for her being was enough to keep me at the mercy of the hands of unrequited love.

I smoked and then showered. I felt the warm, soapy water cleanse my skin. I felt restored and comfortable. I didn't care too much for how I looked, but I dressed with the purpose of looking clean. I powered through three glasses of wine as I smoked another cigarette. Time to hit the streets.

As I exited my apartment building, my cell phone rang. It was an unknown number. I didn't answer it. If it were of any importance, a message would be left. For a moment, a broken moment, I thought it could be Soledad calling me. I let the thought evaporate as I walked into the sun.

The afternoon began to mature as I walked by a local gentlemen's club called *The Forbidden Fruit.* I stopped in front of its doors and got a glimpse of my reflection that stared back at me from the entry booth window. He was not a complete stranger to me today. I approached the window. Seated at the counter, there was a young, thin, French looking girl with dark auburn hair flowing past her shoulders and a small diamond nose ring. She had her head down with her attention fixed like a cat on what looked like a science textbook. She didn't look up at me right away, but I could see she had clear green eyes that were complimented by her dark eyebrows. I knocked on the window. She looked up and gave a semi-smirk as I stood there. I was never one for gentlemen's clubs, but I thought that this was a place where I could find company without being robbed of my solitude. I paid the entrance fee, and she gave someone a signal to let me in then returned silently to her anatomy book.

The door opened, and I stared into a dark, bottomless pit of sweet despair. A burly man stepped into the doorframe and waved me in. I entered. The sunlight evaporated at my feet in front of me as the door slowly shut behind me. I turned the corner of the dark red draped hallway as my nose stiffened with the smell of baby powder and booze. The place was crowded with patrons ranging in age from "skipped lecture" to "avoiding his wife's mother" all the way up to "grandpa's day out."

There was a platinum haired girl dancing around the pole center stage with a crowd seated around her throwing their loneliness at her feet in the form of dollar bills. A couple of other dancers were walking and talking, interacting with the crowd. Through the red neon stage lights I was able to find an open seat at the bar. The bartender was a girl that looked far too young to even be at the place, walked over to me.

"What are you having tonight handsome?"

"Whiskey, neat. No, wait...gin and tonic, please. We'll keep it light for now."

She spun around, and as she did so, I looked at the reflection in the mirror that served as a backdrop to the bottles along the wall. I put a cigarette between my lips. She turned back around and slid me my drink. I took a sip; it was nice and stiff with a splash of lime.

I took a gulp as I grew annoyed by the shitty glam rock that was blaring for the dancer. Everyone's attention was focused center stage, but not mine. My attention belonged to the glass in front of me. The bartender leaned back against the counter facing me with her arms crossed. She too, seemed to offer her attention to the feline that absorbed the dense air of the place. She glanced at me as I gulped down the gin and tonic and caressed it with my eyes as I placed it down. She walked over to me and grabbed the glass.

"Another?" she asked. I nodded in the affirmative.

She quickly poured me another stiff drink and slid it to me. She must have noticed that I wasn't all that interested at the main event of entertainment that was being offered, for she glanced at the others at the bar but then returned to me.

"You're here just to drink?"

I didn't have an answer to give.

"I can introduce you to any of the girls if you like?" She pointed away from the bar to a tall and curvy blonde that stood at the other end of the bar talking to a venerable soul. "She's popular and nice," she added.

"No thank you. Appreciate the thought though." I gave her a pathetic smile and finished my drink. She grabbed the bottle of gin and almost filled the glass with it, topping it off with a splash of tonic and a slice of lime.

"This one's on me."

"Not necessary, but thank you."

She leaned back against the bar and made herself as comfortable as possible. I sat there, cigarette and drink in hand, facing the mirrors. I could see that only I was questioning my attendance, and that, not only did I have my back towards the crowd, but they also had their backs to me. Not once did I again glance at the reflection in the mirror. I didn't really have an interest in the naked beauty that was just a few feet behind me.

Two or three drinks had passed until the burly man finally approached me as I sat at the bar.

"You have to spend some money to stay here; be a gentleman." I laughed at his remark. He didn't like that. I could tell because he gave me a look as if I just went down on his sister. "I'm serious, you can't just stay at the bar."

Just then a girl approached us. She placed her hand on my shoulder as she stood by me.

"It's okay," she said. "He'll keep me company."

The security guard had no choice but to excuse himself. She took a seat that had just opened up right next to me. I didn't turn around and just kept facing the bar. She sat there and let out a sigh.

"How are you doing?"

"Okay. Yourself?"

"Fantastic, want to buy me a drink?" I finished off my drink and waved the bartender over.

"I'll have another gin and tonic...and a ginger ale for her."

Both women laughed as if they hadn't laughed all night. The bartender slid my drink over and slid the nameless dame her ginger ale. She took a sip and looked at me.

"Thank you."

"Don't mention it, you have this round right?"

"You're a charmer aren't you?" she jibed in a dry tone laced with charm. "Can I interest you in a private dance?" she proposed as I gulped my drink.

"No thanks. I was just about to leave. I don't think your friend likes me very much."

She tossed back her hair in response. "Don't mind him; he's a softy. What do you do?"

I finished off my drink and slid it to the bartender once more; she refilled it.

"I'm a writer...or used to be."

"You don't sound sure of yourself."

"I'm not. What do you do?"

She slid her seat closer to me and arched her back, showing off her chest. "We can go behind the curtains, and I can show you?"

"Thank you, but I don't think I'd be worth your while. There's plenty of…"

Just then, the shitty glam rock ended, and the disc jockey started spitting on the microphone. Some jazz started playing on the loudspeakers, the kind that would be played at a cabaret. I turned my attention to the stage for the first time.

"Everyone please welcome to the stage. The lovely *Ella*!"

Her walk onto the stage was as sensual as a kiss but as deadly as the venom of lust. She had legs that were as everlasting as sin; she was pale as a ghost with dark hair, dark eyebrows and dark eyes. All I could do was stare. The music had more of an effect on me, for I didn't expect a slow jazz tune with an accordion. As she twirled around on the stage, her curves broke the stage fog that obscured everything but rays of light and the radiant waves of her hair. The crowd got silent; the seats at the front row were quickly filled, but at the feet of the succubus, the spectators transformed into dogs, howling and growling with their eyes and opened mouths. Even my drinking buddy dancer became silent and attentive as the glow in her eyes remarked on the lustful charm that Ella possessed.

As she continued to captivate her pack, Ella shed her top, and the oxygen in the room vanished. She revealed herself completely as I sipped my gin. I looked down for a moment as I placed a cigarette back between my lips. I looked back up to see that her back was arched while she leaned against the pole. I looked at her eyes but wanted to be able to peer into her eyes. She made her way around the stage, torturing the wild animals that sat at her mercy. As she made her way around the stage, her eyes locked with mine. She didn't smile, nor did I. I couldn't read her gaze. Everyone's head turned as she swayed her body. But hers didn't; she kept staring at me, and with each second that passed, I was cascading into the eyes of the lovely demon. She was a deadly goddess of lust and attention. I felt alone at the fact that only I noticed it in her eyes. I was convinced that I, too, was drawn to her and able to recognize her beauty but was immune to whatever charm she had. As she looked into my eyes, time stood still. I knew she knew that I was unreachable. Without taking her eyes away from mine, she bent down in front of some guy that wasn't immune and picked up his pride. The song faded out as she stood up; still focusing on me, she finally broke out a smirk. Her worshippers stood up, clapped, and cheered wildly but not I. She never looked away as all I did was down my drink, and then gave my back to her and her howling dogs.

I looked at her reflection in the mirror for only a moment, paid my tab, and headed towards the door. There was a line of yipping mongrels waiting to take her for a private show. I could feel her dark eyes burning the back of my neck as I turned the corner into the red draped hallway, howls fading behind me as I exited onto the streets.

The sky was dark, and the moon was barely rising. I lit a smoke and walked down the street with the crescent moon on my shoulders. I was by my place but wasn't ready to call it a night. I wandered and ended up in front of *Soledad's Books and Coffee*. My heart felt a slight break, like when a beautiful stranger passes you going the other way on the sidewalk. I looked in through the window. There wasn't a single movement in the place. I finished my cigarette and yielded to my courage. I entered the store

It was dim, not quite how I remembered it to be, but it was lifeless as usual. No one was seen or heard. The books had collected dust on the shelves. I slowly walked about the store, staining my nostrils with the sullen odor that now seemed all too familiar. No coffee was brewed. I stood in the middle of the store and studied the place with a sadness only a writer would know. I lit a cigarette. The smoke twirled in the air with the dry and sullen scent of forsakenness. The ashy tears of my cigarette fell lifeless on the floor.

I left. I once again looked in through the window. I looked inside in hopes of finding someone, some soul just wandering about. I hoped in vain.

On the walk home I passed a boarded up little store. This is where Miss Remedios had her little shop. It wasn't all that sad looking, the place boarded up that is. It was unquestionably sadder with a little old lamenting lady in the middle of the shop with baskets full of unwanted flowers. I heard a voice behind me.

"Hello and good evening, young man. I'm delighted to see you again." It was Miss Remedios.

"Buenas tardes," I said. "Miss Remedios, it is I who is delighted to see you. What brings you around here at this time of night?"

She turned away from me and laid her sad eyes on the boarded up place that used to be her livelihood.

"Just going on a walk. Vicente and I would try to walk most evenings," she explained without looking away from the boards covering the shop.

"I was just going to get a cup of coffee and go on a walk myself. Would you join me? I, too, could use some company."

She smiled, "Sure."

I offered my arm for her to hold as I attempted to guide her away from her painful memories.

We walked down the street towards the café—the first one I invited Soledad to. As we strolled down the street, a nostalgic smile came to my face as the streetlights followed us, turning on one by one. She turned her little head towards me.

"Have you had a nice and quiet evening? I like nice and quiet evenings."

"Yes, for the most part. I just came from a gentlemen's club."

She chuckled as she turned her eyes up at me, but her head remained facing frontwards.

"But it was reposeful," I said. "It proved to be uneventful."

"Did you have a good time?"

"Not really, no."

"That's interesting. Most men at your young age have a ball at those places."

"I could see why, but I didn't. It felt...lonely. I didn't really want to talk to anyone, but I wanted a form of company, but it didn't feel right. I found myself feeling more alone than I originally did when I walked in."

We came up to the café. I held the door open for her as she continued to speak her mind.

"If you are looking for love, I can guarantee you, you won't find it there." She entered the café, and I followed. We sat at a booth that was by the front window. "I assume the girl you were mourning over hasn't come back into your life?"

I was embarrassed; she must have known I lied from the start. It was true I still mourned my mother, however, I hadn't had the courage to tell a stranger that I was hurting over a girl who was part of my life for so little time. Only enough time to make a handful of memories, a handful of painful memories that I kept beneath my lapel.

"No, she hasn't," I replied. A waitress came to us. Remedios just ordered a cup of coffee with milk; I ordered the same.

"Love—it is as painful as it is beautiful."

Our coffees arrived. As she spoke to me, my phone rang again. It was another unknown caller. I felt rude, so I rejected the call and gave her my attention. She stirred the milk into her coffee.

"There is no shame in loving, even if it is love that is not returned. Did you love her?"

"I don't know," I said. She just gave me a look like she knew again that I was lying. "Yes...yes I did." I realized I was self-effacing although I was sure what I was and how I felt.

"How long had you known her?"

"A few days," I smiled sheepishly.

"Seems rather quick for you to fall in love, don't you think?" she prodded.

I sipped my coffee and placed my cigarettes on the black and white checkered tabletop.

"I don't believe there has ever been a girl with whom I've had a ten-minute conversation with and didn't fall in love. But, the heartbreaks I'll carry for the rest of my life."

"What made you fall in love with her so much that you love her even though she didn't return your love?"

I stayed quiet. Like a thief in the night, Soledad stole my love. Not only my love for her, but for the sea, for music and for the essence of anything that is beauty. Without this love, I cannot live. The absurdity of love became even more profound in that moment. The coffee itself became extra bitter after that realization.

"Remedios, it's because I have a natural melancholic state. I dwell a lot, too much. Then I look at the beautiful things that life has to offer, the little things, sunsets, the moon, the sea, and then I remember her essence and her eyes. Then I realize within all the loneliness that I am a bohemian, I am the sea, and I am love."

I got her to smile, a full on smile for the first time that night. She looked down at her steaming cup of coffee.

"You remind me so much of my poor Vicente. He was artistic, a painter and a poet. He was a tortured man; he could never fight off his demons. But all he could ever do was love. He loved me; I am proud to say I loved him. He was one of those rare spirits who could love everyone and everything but himself. Much like you, I am guessing. He loved the dark starry nights. The blue and gray colored mountains on a linen canvas and the hot summer days often reminded him of his own discontent. He had sad infant like eyes; he looked at the world with such curiosity and humanity. I knew it tortured him even more to know that. Much like people, flowers and animals suffered as well." She drank her coffee and continued. "I don't judge you; only you know if you're in love. And if it's unrequited love, I hope you know it is worth it. Not everyone is capable of loving, for not all are capable of dominating their grand emotions. These folks leave me quite cold, like a bleak wind."

My mind staggered with the gravity of sudden consciousness. It hadn't occurred to me that our emotions *weren't* our enemies. I always had a hate for my emotions. I didn't hate life; I endured all the beatings I could take. We have to keep answering the bell for the next round. More often than not, we don't recognize our valor. Too many people just exist in their own lives and do not dare to live— perhaps out of boredom or fear. But, with a knockout punch from Miss Remedios, through her clear, mother's eyes, I saw a blinding light. We must have courage to live, and we must not fear love.

She looked at her cup and then returned her attention to me. "This is a cold world. You can't carry the weight of the world on your shoulders or heart. Not because of its mass, but because humanity will not only be oblivious of your humanity, but the mere fact of your humanity will go unappreciated."

"Truer words have never been spoken," I concurred.

"In the little time I have spent with you, I feel closer to my late husband—may he rest in peace. I feel closer to him now than I ever did when he was alive. He wasn't a cold person; he had a broken but grand heart. He loved and could be loved, but his tortures banned him to his loneliness. This world...wasn't meant for the beautiful ones."

I sat speechless, sipped my coffee and just soaked in her wisdom. I watched her hands as she cupped her palms and fingers around her cup. The creases of her tan but gray vellum hands told more of what she had been through than the words falling from her sagacious lips. Her eyes began to tear as she tried to hide her yawns.

"May I walk you home? It is dark out, and my mother would scold me for not walking you home."

She nodded and led the way. We didn't talk as we walked. We both enjoyed the silent company; that is a hard thing to find and share with another person. I never feared silence between my companions and I. Everything that could be said had been said, and there was no reason to disrupt the amiable silence with empty words.

We reached an apartment complex. As she entered the front gate, I noticed a small garden of flowers along the gate. She turned to face me; I felt her eyes on me as I looked down at the flowers. There were daisies and daffodils. Without a word, I reached down and plucked three yellow daffodils and handed them to her. I finally broke the silence.

"Gracias, Dama; thank you for your wisdom, but most of all for your company."

"No, thank you, Juanito. It was a nice reminder that there are people who are capable of grand emotions. Buenas noches, mijo."

I nodded and watched her disappear in the shadows. I lit a cigarette and went on my way.

When I arrived home, it was still early, so I started drinking my wine, and it was consumed quite quickly. I opened up a bottle of liquor and a Benze inhaler. I hadn't written, and I was supposed to be a writer. Drugs and alcohol famously serve as creative lubricants—merely a means to quickly achieve a constant stream of consciousness. However, not ready to face the reproachful gaze of my typewriter, I once more left my studio for a night out.

The walk was chilly and quiet. The clouds of smoke that I left curling behind me were lonesome clouds looking for company. Once at the store, I couldn't decide if I wanted liquor or wine; wine is certainly fine, but liquor is notably quicker.

The clerk watched me with suspicion. Not that it was his concern, but after my release, I was supposed to remain sober, but I had grown bored with having a clear mind. I was there for a bottle of liquor and a good time with a benny, and a benny with a good time.

I instinctually picked up a bottle of Four Roses but then felt a stab of disconsolate whiplash, so I put it back, grabbed a bottle of Jimmy B Devil's Cut instead, and a Benze inhaler. It would be a boys' night out for Johnny, Jimmy and Benny. The clerk gave me a sanctimonious smirk as he rang up my friends; there was nothing wrong with him that a fifty-cent raise wouldn't fix.

I left the store and opened the bottle of whiskey for a snort. The people heading to the soulless clubs to get loaded also passed their judgement on me. I could feel it and see it in their eyes, along with the way they turned their heads as they neared. No one crossed the street to avoid me outright, but they castigated me with their reproachful backs.

It didn't really matter to me; there's no difference between a homeless wino and a drunkard who pisses himself in his mansion. We are all mortal; we're all going to die. Some die with honor, and that is noble. Others die with the illusion of dying with dignity, and I am sympathetic towards these people. Yes, we are all going to die, and nothing will matter, for we die without a social class, without pride, and without mercy. I'd like to say that we die without judgment but that, too, is an illusion. The soul of a martyr—who could also be referred to as a victim of suicide—can testify to this claim. Mental illness is blamed for the death of a suicide victim, while the lack of support from others remains blameless. This, too, has a blue side; a victim of suicide leaves behind the potential support along with any drop of dignity. No matter how we leave this world, it is never beautiful, and it is always brutal. One can die with their loved ones close by or on a bed of roses, but assuredly, dignity died long before that last breath. Dying without dignity does not bother me, and if there is a maker, only it will know the truth of my death.

Half a bottle of whiskey and blocks walked in the wrong direction; I found myself in front of the Cathedral. The synchronicity of my thoughts and location transmogrified the smoky taste of my whiskey into tar. I stood at the foot of the steps and looked up at the monolith.

I sparked a cigarette as I sat on the steps and popped the cotton from the inhaler into my bottle of whiskey. I didn't want to step inside the church but couldn't resist its summons. I went inside.

The heavy door slowly closed behind me, and the chiaroscuro lighting served as a dramatic backdrop to my position of seeking amnesty. The only light sources were those of the golden candlelight that surrounded the altar and a beam of a pale golden color that drenched half of the giant crucifix. The statue of everyone's beloved Jesus was half in shadow. His head hung weary to one side away from the light. The light shined off his ribs and his pronounced cheekbone. He was gaunt like a raven. I walked closer to the altar.

Blacker than black were the shadows at the foot of the altar. A clear line of light and shadow was between the altar and myself. I thought of my mother and her great faith. She had always found great peace here.

I realized that if I were to die before having love in my heart, it would be due to suicide. I'd have a graceless fall to earth with broken wings. The only thing I had to offer here on earth was my spirit. I could attempt to offer my dreams and skies just to be able to feel the vigorous heat of my mother's peace. There's only an end; everything has an end.

I closed my eyes after another sip of whiskey, and I saw myself flying over the earth and the seas. Nostalgia is murderous in the depths of untold stories that exist under the sun.

I walked out of the Cathedral; nothing changed.

Impulsively, I walked to *Soledad's Books and Coffee*. As I arrived at the bookstore, I had just less than a third of my bottle left, and the benny in the whiskey was starting to strut and flex in my bloodstream. I looked through the window. Nothing. The lights were on, so I entered.

I stepped inside and the only thing that could be heard was the creaking hardwood floor grinding with every step I took. The gentle sigh of relief from the books on the shelves pollinated the air with fantastic desperation.

I found myself in the philosophical fiction section, and I was scanning the books when I heard footsteps. Fear, or the damn benze inhaler, yanked a knot in my intestines. Anxiety fogged my head, and I stood silently and steady on the balls of my feet. The silence was uncomfortable for the first time in my life. It grew denser, like the lawn of an abandoned house; I couldn't tell the difference between the thick green and tan grass and the rough weeds that had declared war on the land. For a nanosecond, I half hoped, half worried that it might be Soledad approaching, but the thought was quickly cast aside.

The harps of emotion, along with an offbeat longing, accompanied the fast drumming in my chest. I took three long steps to the end of the aisle. I took out my bottle of whiskey; quickly and silently, I drank the rest of it. My stomach burned from the whiskey and the menthol from the inhaler cotton. I screwed the bottle cap back on and went to place the bottle in my coat pocket. I missed, and it fell towards the floor. The drums were louder as the jungle swing beat got faster and faster. I stood there as I turned to see the bottle spinning and twirling as it tumbled downward. It crashed against the hardwood floor and spun. The sound of the glass bottle spinning on the floor didn't cease until I placed my foot on its neck. The bookstore was silent as death.

I picked up the bottle, stood back up, and placed the bottle on the bookcase.

"Hello?" A young and startled female voice purred out like a cat. The jungle jazz drumbeat that was pounding in my head and heart came to a sudden stop. The echo and sustain from the drums reverberated throughout my body.

I stepped out into the open floor of the bookstore. It was an unfamiliar young lady with pale, creamy skin that covered her pear shaped form. She, too, had sad eyes. I found her to be quite lovely in her dolor. There's something about women everyone should notice. When a woman is sad, she is lovelier than ever. When sadness is in the eyes of a woman, she becomes honest and holds no secrets.

She stood there, waiting for me to break the silence. Sensually, my eyes feathered her figure like a painter would feather their brush on a nude painting. She had an unconventionally lovely nose, like that of a boxer with a slight bump. She placed one of her hands on her hip and slightly slanted her stance. I noticed her bracelet that glittered under the dim light and a big silver flower ring she wore on her middle finger. The petals of the ring blossomed out, stretching out, covering joints on her index and ring finger. She raised her sienna and umber glazed eyebrows at me.

"Apologies for the noise, I didn't think it would startle anyone."

She smiled, and that flattered her sad eyes. The benze started to fondle my senses. A cool, tingling sensation was felt on my temples to the top of my head. All I could do was smile. I couldn't tell if it was my libido or just the drug induced euphoria taking over.

"It's okay," she shrugged. "I didn't think anyone was in here, unfortunately, we don't get too many people in here anymore. It's a shame."

"It is a shame indeed."

"Glad to see someone who still has an interest in books; it's like too many people try to find balance or entertainment in other things these days."

"They can't find what they're looking for because they aren't looking for it," I preached.

"What is it you're looking for?" she coaxed with a glint in her clover honey eyes.

"I'm conflicted, to tell the truth. What is it that most people look for? Faith? Companionship? Or maybe just a simple explanation for how to deal with our human condition?"

She took a couple steps towards me. My lungs filled with cool air. She got within a few feet in front of me and examined the section where I was standing.

"Hmm, Philosophical Fiction. Possibly a good place to start." Her pink *Lolita* lips were soft rose petals that you just want to touch with fingertips or lips. She gave a surprised smile and laughed as she pointed at the empty bottle I had placed on the bookcase. "Is that yours?" Her muted brown eyes searched mine

"Nope," I lied amiably. She looked at the bottle and then back at me. I laughed, "I didn't think there was anyone else around that would like a drink." I placed my hand over my chest and nodded in mock apology.

She smiled; this time she smiled and showed her pearl white teeth. She shook her head "no," in polite exasperation.

"So...old dead white guys and a bottle of whiskey with a weird piece of cotton inside...what are you, depressed?"

"I don't know...maybe."

"Poor Baby..." It is amazing how much sarcasm can be forgiven when it comes from lips as lovely as hers.

I stepped forward and extended my hand. "I'm Johnny, Johnny Espiritu."

Without letting go of my hand, she turned her head to the side and gave a frown of curiosity. Her forehead wrinkled and her eyebrows scrunched together.

"Johnny Espiritu? The writer?"

"Yes."

"Interesting to see you here all alone. I've read some of your work."

I looked at our hands that were still clenched together.

"What did you think of it?"

She finally let go of my hand and placed her hand on her hip. "I liked your writing," she said rather slowly, and then added, "It's interesting, dark, well humored and perverted in a beautiful way."

Mildly flattered, and more than mildly aroused, I took a step back and leaned back on the bookcase expectantly.

"What have you been working on?"

"Nothing," I confided.

"Really?"

"Really."

She leaned back on the bookcase in front of me. I tried hard not to stare at her form, but it was difficult to resist. The white button up shirt that she wore strained against her voluptuous cleavage. I wanted to envelop her, breath in her perfume, kiss her rose petal mouth. There is a comfort in sharing intimacy with a stranger. I didn't know her, but she apparently knew me. She slid down against the bookcase and sat down with her legs crossed. I followed suit.

"I figured it should be easy for someone like you to be able to write whenever you want."

"Not exactly. Being a writer sucks. At least, it sucks for me."

She seemed shocked at my response. She crossed her arms and probed, "Why's that?"

"It doesn't really suck…" I hedged. I was starting to squirm under her scrutiny.

"You don't have anything to say through writing?"

"Nothing worth saying...at the moment," I confessed. There was too much truth in those words. Mentally, I stomped on the neck of my insecurity.

She laughed, "Why are you so somber? Your writings might be dark, but you seem very conscience of your surroundings. Your words have a way of showing the beautiful facets of the ugliest scenarios. I would think that you would be more optimistic in your outlook."

"That might be the problem," I countered, "Finding beauty is only possible if one continually looks for the grotesque, and I find much of existence to be quite monstrous."

"That's a gift though," she remarked, "to see the world with such a keen sense of contrast. I think I'd like to spend a day with you and pick your brain."

"That's not that great of an idea; I don't mean to offend you. Not to sound cliché, but, it's not you, it's me, honestly."

She was quick with her reply, "Let me guess, Mrs. Espiritu would get angry?" She puckered her lips in a delightful moue.

"There's no Mrs."

"Hmm," she puzzled, "where does all the love in your work come from then?" She grinned with bewitching impudence. I delighted in her bold and straightforward manner. She sat there with her arms crossed, a reproachful librarian with a gorgeous rack. The air became thick with the perfume of intimated lust.

I leaned across the aisle, placed my hand on the side of her neck, pulled her close, and kissed her as we lay down on the floor. Books fell off the shelf, spectators to one of life's great pleasures. The Libertines would have been proud.

She sighed, reposed, as I sat up and lit a cigarette.

"My toes are numb," she purred through her breath. Lying back down next to her, I proffered her the cigarette to her lips. She inhaled deeply with her eyes closed and released another sigh of pleasure, this time for the nicotine.

"I ought to get going," I said reluctantly. She didn't respond as I got up and started getting dressed. She sat up, still naked, grabbed me by my belt buckle and hoisted herself up. I wrapped one arm around her, holding the burning cherry in my other hand away from her tousled hair and kissed her again.

"See you later?" she asked. I smiled, placed the cigarette between her lips, gave her a peck on her forehead, got dressed, and gave her a half bow as I turned and walked towards the door.

Upon exiting, I lit another smoke and walked to the liquor store halfway between my apartment and I. The sky was black, accompanied by a few gray clouds masking the stars and draping the moon in a velvet haze. The store was about to close as I approached, but I made it in the door just as the clerk was walking up to lock it. He rolled his eyes but let me in.

"I'll be quick," I promised.

Quick I was, for, a few seconds later I walked out with another bottle of Devil's Cut that was sure to put me over. The euphoria was just what I needed. I felt as if angels through clouds of harmony were carrying me. I continued the walk home feeling disorientated. I got lost. I reached a park in the middle of this metropolitan crazed place.

There was a small, paved pathway that slowly disappeared as it narrowed into the shadows from the trees. I noticed a golden light that was on top of a post towards the middle of the park. I sipped my whiskey and let the wind guide me towards the light. I thought I heard a violinist as I got closer, but I couldn't see anyone. Right before the lamppost, there was a wooden bench. I sat down. I did hear a violinist, but then the music suddenly stopped. As my eyes adjusted to the lack of light, I went from looking up at the stars down to another bench further into the obscurity of the park.

I noticed golden highlights on what I made out to be two silhouettes that were sitting closely together on the bench. It was a young couple, maybe in their late teens, embraced in each other's arms. Out of the shadows in front of them walked out an old, worn out man who wore a heavy coat. He got closer, and as he did, he took notice of me sitting there alone amongst clouds of smoke. He smiled at me. As he glowed under the lamppost, I noticed the violin in his hand.

"Was that you playing?"

His eyes lit up, but it could have also been the light from the lamppost. "Yes sir," he responded in an accent unknown to me. He looked back at the young lovers. "I tried to play for them," he said as he lifted his violin closer to his chest, "but the young man refused."

"That's unfortunate," I said, "romanticism is a dying art, a dying flower and a dying life." I didn't realize that I was speaking out loud. I was under the impression my thoughts were my own, but then I noticed the violinist nodding his head in grave agreement.

I might be alone, but you don't need a love near you to dedicate a song to them or to dedicate a song to love itself. I took out some cash and handed it to him.

He demurred, "To play for you, sir? It's too much."

"Please," I said, "Take it and play."

He didn't move. I placed the cash on the bench and grabbed the whiskey, took a drink and then offered him the bottle. With hesitation, he grabbed the bottle from my hands and lifted it up to his nose. Finally, he took a small swig and handed it back to me. I grabbed the cash and offered it to him once more. He took it, placed it in his coat pocket, bowed his head, lifted his violin to his chin and rested it on his shoulder. He played the strings with his bow ever so gently. The mellifluous croon of the violin sheltered me as the strings serenaded into the thieving wind. He played *Dark Eyes*.

He ended the song, and I drowned him in applause along with the smoke from my cigarette that twirled around him and his violin. We both had another drink, and he continued to play. My eyes, like the trees, swayed around the darkness that surrounded us. As if it were autumn, all the leaves looked like flowers gliding down to the ground. My eyes wandered to the young lovers on the other bench. Naturally, their attention was completely focused on the twisting and twirling of their tongues.

Out of the shadows came another dark figure that walked by the young lovers. The figure was clearly carrying a white bucket that hung from its shoulder. I felt the heat from the cigarette blush my nose and lips as I saw the dark figure hold out a flower to the young man. I couldn't hear anything, but the young man responded to the shadowed figure. Rejection is bitter, no matter what you are offering. The shadowed figure placed the flower back into the bucket and walked towards the violinist and I.

As the person made it closer to the lamppost, I realized it was the older gentleman from whom I had bought flowers before. I sipped my whiskey and raised my hand to greet him, "Señor, good evening!"

He stopped in his tracks and studied me. I could see him clearly now as he grinned with joy.

"Señor, good evening to you as well. What brings you to the park at this hour?"

"Just enjoying some music and the nighttime breeze."

The song ended as I drank some more. I offered it over to the violinist; he obliged and handed the bottle back. I took another sip and held it out to the florist, "How's business tonight?"

"Not too good, Señor. I offered a flower to the young man, but he is not a romantic."

I glanced over to the couple. They still embraced each other, but the young man was glaring over in our direction. I lit another smoke as we passed the bottle around. I was drunk, and the violinist was turning a bright red under the golden light. I grabbed some cash and handed it to the florist. I stood up and inspected the flowers he had. I picked out some white ones; I don't know what kind of flowers they were, but I handed them to the florist.

"Take these to the girl over there."

He looked nervous. He didn't take hold of the flowers as he looked over to the young couple. The young lovers were once again kissing in the dark.

"But...she is with a fellow," he exclaimed.

"It's okay; tell her they are from me. She deserves them."

He hesitated for another moment. I handed him the whiskey, and he drank some courage. He took a deep breath and exhaled it slowly. He took the flowers from my hand, turned and slowly walked towards the young couple.

As he approached the couple, they turned toward him. The girl looked over in my direction as the florist explained something and handed her the flowers. I had no idea whether or not she could see me, but I couldn't help but smile. The feeling got better when she took the flowers into her hand and waved in my direction. Her man just turned to me and held out his middle finger.

The florist came back with a joy that lit up the night. I had another round with the florist and the violinist and bid them farewell. The smell of the flowers perfumed the air around me, much like Soledad had once long ago. I walked out of the park.

I got home soon thereafter with Soledad on my mind and the hounds of memory and desire on my trail. I switched on a light and walked over to my kitchen counter and grabbed my corkscrew, lit a smoke and spun some Tom Waits on the record player. The wine was sweet but strong, like the love for someone who is oblivious to its existence. The smokes were unfiltered and toasted; they felt just right. The benny was still going strong—an old Desoto on the road with no particular place to go. The music was smooth and sexy. I went over to my typewriter and played the keys like a piano. I was unsteady, drunk, high and alone. The room was still dim, so I went over to my nightstand and switched on the lamp. As ash fell off my cigarette and tumbled down, I noticed a cockroach on my nightstand. The thing should have been afraid, but it remained still. I was disgusted upon seeing it there but recalled the state it was seeing me in.

It's shiny, black, vibrant, brown and yellow body glistened and reflected the light. It faced me without movement. It hadn't moved so I thought it might be dead, but its little eyes blinked and moved about, studying me.

"I must kill it," I said to myself. "I must rid it of its foul appearance and flush it down." I wrestled off my shoe, and it didn't move, but its antennae swayed in an invisible breeze. Slowly and steadily, I studied its movements so I would know when to strike. It flinched as it saw me raise my shoe above my head. The music went into double time as the suspense grew between this bug and I. I felt the beads of sweat on my nose. One bead dripped off. I looked into its eyes as its antennae continued to waver suspiciously. I lowered the shoe.

I didn't have a reason to kill it. It hadn't done a thing except to merely exist—much like a person; most people merely exist. Man is not at fault for living, man is at fault for not living, or not truly living. I let it live. I tossed the shoe onto the floor as the static of the record player filled the room.

I was filled without something fantastic, something horrifying, but fantastic. Like a ghost, through all the static, I heard the chirping of a cricket at my windowsill. I felt cold. I picked up the needle off the record. The cockroach stayed still as I started to down my wine. The room and my head were a blur. The cricket chirped louder. I felt sick but lit another smoke. It made me gag, so I drank more wine as I sat up. I threw up in a small tin waste can next to the nightstand. I fell back on the futon. The smell of roses settled my stomach. The chirps of the cricket bounced off my eardrums, and I had nothing left. I had had enough. I was tired, sick, and sick and tired. I needed more wine, but I had had enough. I closed my eyes, searching for sleep and darkness.

~~~~~~

To me, eternal slumber was now a reality. It was a dream within a dream. I was peacefully lying with my eyes gradually adjusting to the glorious light that bathed me. I was lying on green grass that was greener that any pigment that yellow and blue could make. My head was pristine like the sea. Clear of all distorted views and ideals. My roots were as deep in the ground as a redwood trees. Like the tree, I stood tall with my branches wide open; arms wide open like death when she greets you after a well lived life. With a life full of love and appreciation. The sun was comfortably hot, like those of an enchanted spring day, like the grandiose days of my boyhood. The moon was high in the sky. The sky was split in two, split right down the middle. Right down the middle of the sky was an oily blend of blue and black. The two skies gradually blended into one another. On one side, puffy, soft, cotton candy popcorn clouds slowly passed by the sun. On the other side, the sky was black, enamored with a silver full moon made of cheese and sprinkled with radiant stardust. The breeze whistled a hymn in the wind as the birds harmonized. I was relieved of all human tortures. It was a world without a trace of bloody wars or stains of resistance. Hunger was nonexistent. Nothing was answered, but it didn't matter. There weren't any questions in search of an answer.

There weren't any angels or saints present, so I lacked the confidence to call the place heaven. The air was a virgin, untouched by human hands, and unpolluted by man's greed and restless lives. A seraphim breeze was the oxygen that filled my lungs. It purified my breath and my blood.

All worries known to mankind were evaporated; those of social pressures and pleasure seeking were evaporated and converted into rain—a rain that was nothing more than angelic tears of joy. The days were more than a dream. Hope seemed to be but an extra bag that wasn't needed on the train. Hope didn't exist, for it wasn't needed.

To be here is for life, in itself, to be a romance. To love, sing, to be a tree or to flap your wings high in the sky. Where the green leaves of a grand summer were to be your companions and a pillow to rest your head. Time was infinite, although you didn't have time to care.

The sea must have been close. I heard the rumbles of the baritone and soprano waves splash and crash against what I imagined to be numberless golden grains of hot sand. The time under the sun and moon wasn't to be measured. The day and night had no beginning or end.

I walked down a path where the leaves were painted yellow and orange by autumn. Along the trees of autumn, I hiked on the edge of winter. The umber and yellow leaves that ornamented the ground flirted with the bleak, white snows that were on the opposite side. To my left were the fall trees with their cool and glistening dew, and on my right, the depths of winter with its chills freezing all loneliness with its snow that covered the linen dirt.

At the end of this path I was greeted by summer and its sea. Pearl flakes winked their eyes at me from the surface of the water. I ran onto the hot sand that tickled my soft toes until I dove into the warm sea. She wasn't as savage as we had come to know her on earth. She, too, was a virgin, untouched by the hands of sinners and undaunted by their intentions. She was crystal clear and filled with life. She wasn't lonely. Schools of myriad fish swam in all directions. I, too, was a fish. My body absorbed the oxygen from the water and had no need to break the surface. Rays of light broke through and shined themselves to inveigle me to catch them.

I swam deeper and deeper to the vibrant coral forest that was home to life, as much as it served as tombstones for the innocent. Everything was undisturbed. Existence was poetry. It was a life without crime and without the aging of time.

Nothing was human. There was no need or want for the likes of smokes or wine. This place had and gave substance to art. Everything: the sky, the sea, the day and night were all elegant classical oil paintings.

I broke the surface and saw the day sky turn a heavenly red. What I thought to be just the sun setting was a mere cycle of a continuous sun setting and rising. I swam back to shore guided by mermaids. I viewed them without lust or temptation. Their magnificent forms glided through the water effortlessly. They blew kisses to me as I reached the land.

I threw myself on the sand facing skyward. I studied the combination of the blended day and night sky and was witness to countless expired, falling stars and birds flew freely in the sky.

I walked back from the summer, through the path of winter and fall, until I found myself back in the spring. I was conscious of the soft blades of grass beneath my wet feet as I walked up a little hill shaded by giant trees. I found some shade there, surrounded by yellow daffodils and white daisies. I lay down on a bed of grass between the flowers and let the breeze dry me off. The daffodils and daisies turned to face me and blushed my cheeks with their radiant scents.

I shut my eyes and took a deep breath. There was only one thought in my mind. My funeral.

I always swore that I would not have a funeral because no one would come. It took place in a giant adobe chapel. I was in a simple wooden box with a line of people waiting to pay their respects. The Mariachis were playing Rancheras while everyone in attendance sang along. There wasn't an empty seat, and the doors of the chapel were left open for those who could not fit inside.

The altar was adorned with golden orange *Cempazuchitls*, marigolds, and everyone held yellow daffodils. The person in the very front row, dressed in black and in a veil of sorrow too dense to penetrate, was Soledad herself. With a room full of people, she stood alone. No one was to recognize her or to comfort her. Whether her tears were of regret or mourning, it didn't matter. I imagined her eyes drowning and her cheeks and nose a muted red. I had no idea why she was at my funeral or why she was suffering. I thought that in death one leaves everything: love, pain and loneliness to name a few. In death, loneliness is left without a companion. Soledad herself was lonely.

The mariachis played their final song at the chapel as everyone walked up to my coffin and filled it with the daffodils. Only my pale, wrinkled face and some grey hair was left clear of adornments. Someone closed the coffin but I didn't know who. Everyone applauded when the mariachis rang out their final note, and I was cleansed and enclosed in applause along with cries of love.

I was buried on a cliff above the sea. I was to be the lone resting person at that sea. The masses of people surrounded the cliff, and if you would have looked to the back of the crowd, the furthest away looked like little black dots.

The dirt piled up on top of me as some attendees wept and others looked up at the sky. Before they forget me, they'll make their own history. I never kneeled to life, and my soul was not at fault. They will search the rest of their lives for what I always sought. Like me, they will never find it, and they will evaporate and return as rain to drown the world of faith. They will never truly live if they keep searching for a meaning. A meaning doesn't exist; just love what you have and protect it with fire.

I was not afraid to die; life and death should have feared me. I died with love in my heart, and life, nor death, could ever rob me of it. In hours of light and in hours of darkness, in the hours of life, and at the hour of my death, I had loved with a true and beautiful love, much like the sun as he ran away with the moon. This love gives substance to life.

I was completely covered with earth. The sunset was a witness to people leaving. Soledad stood there alone. I was gone; I had gone further than the sun. The mariachis stayed with her and played on. Once the moon had risen above them, she turned and walked away from my grave, and the mariachis followed. She had left me again, but this time I had the sea.

~~~~~~

I came to while my cell phone was ringing— another unknown caller. The sun was high in the sky, and I stood at the edge of a cliff above the sea. The journey taken to get here wasn't even a memory. I hadn't an idea of what had happened or what the night witnessed before I ended up on the sea cliff. Naturally, I had a bottle of red wine and cigarettes. The haze twirled around in my head as I pulled out a smoke and lit it. Three gulps of wine were what I needed to clear my head. I walked towards the edge and looked down. Little pieces of rock crumbled beneath my feet and tumbled all the way down. The tide was high and the mist from the crashing waves wrapped around me. The glistening water blinded me. When I stood still, I felt the immense power of the sea as the crashing of the waves sent an energy up the cliff that wobbled my knees. More wine.

I stood there looking out from the edge of the continent. And then looked back down to the shiny rocks that disappeared at the edge of the water. I spit. Three and a half seconds or so is how long it took for my spit to hit the surface of the water. "That's high enough."

I walked back from the edge and sat down on the ground. Smoked another cigarette and drank wine. My cell phone rang again. It was possibly the same unknown caller. I answered it.

"Hello?"

"Hello?" a female voice responded. I thought it must be Soledad; I felt it in my stomach until the woman continued to speak. "Is this Mr. Espiritu?"

"Yes, speaking." I was annoyed for no particular reason.

"Good afternoon, I hope you are well." I chuckled at her salutation. "My name is Consuelo. I heard that you were in dire need of new representation. Can we speak, or do you prefer to meet?"

"You're hired."

"Really? Just like that? You don't want to hear my offer?"

"There's nothing you can offer that I haven't heard already."

She remained quiet. I felt her disappointment over my tone through her silence. I decided to comfort her.

"Look, I apologize for my rudeness. Right now isn't exactly a good time. If you want the job it's yours. I trust you."

"He didn't say it would be this easy."

"He?"

"Yes," she said, "your old agent, Conor; he said you were a good friend of his and that you were looking for new representation."

I guess Conor was good for something, but I had no desire to hear about him, especially not him calling me a friend. He had never called or asked me out for a cup of coffee; he was a man whose business was his priority—a trait I found offensive in a man.

"The job is yours."

She sounded elated and relieved, "Great! When can I meet you? I'd love to hear about what you have been working on."

"I'm working on something right now; let me call you back." I hung up.

A second later and I was at the cliff, and it was grand. The sun was shining bright, and the vast view of the lovely sea was breathtaking. I gulped my wine and dragged my cigarette. The wind pushed me back, but I managed to look down. The once thunderous waves looked like ripples in a brook that slowly caressed pebbles that were at the edge of the sandy beach.

Time stood still but was simultaneously running out. When one is at such heights, fear is common, but not for me. I felt that I could jump off and fly, even if it was with broken wings. I would soar freely in the wind and under the hot sun in a shower of glorious light.

She called my name. The Sea called my name, and all I could do was hear her. Her depths, her currents and her turmoil were all whispering my name.

The rocks will catch me, and I will be gifted into the Sea, and I'll become hers forever. Things are much simpler in death. Death is certain. "Is life worthy of living?" I asked myself. Only the sun and moon know for certain. I stepped closer to the edge, closer to the edge of the cliff and closer to the edge of a new beginning. Absurdity didn't matter; neither did death.

Perhaps a happy death was the purpose of life? One can be content without happiness. The wind blew strong and then came the fall.

It all happened slowly. The fall was graceful and dynamic. The wind whistled as the tumbling and turning took place. The fall hadn't been broken yet, but the future seemed so close, and the memories were blown away by the wind.

The crash was violent. There was red everywhere, red on the black rocks and in the water. The foam turned a deep maroon, and all the pieces of glass glistened up at me. The bottle of wine took exactly three and a half seconds to hit the rocks and bleed into the water.

I gazed down at the red sea and then up at its horizon. The hot sun felt different to me. It felt the way it felt when I was a boy running around with my brother. The grandest days were those of the sun. And when the moon visited me that evening, in her, I found a loyal companion to wait with me until the sun was to shine again.